LADYBIRD

BELOW THE SALT SERIES
BOOK NINE

ELIZABETH ROSE

FAMILY TREE

<u>Blake Family Tree:</u>

Evan & Eleanor Blake
   <u>Their children, spouses, their kids, and books where you can read about them:</u>

Corbett married (Devon) – Lord of the Blade
   Rook 'twin'(Primrose Ashdown) – A Rose Among Thorns
   Beowulf
   Raven 'twin' (Jonathon Armstrong) – Picking up the Gauntlet
   Sparrow
   Tolin (Kit Baker)
   Daegel

Wren (Storm MacKeefe) – Lady Renegade
   Renard – Lady Renegade

Lark (Dustin Styles) – Love Letters for Lady Lark
Florie (different father)
Elspeth
Finlay (Seen in Highland Chronicles)
Hawke (Phoebe MacNab) – Highland Storm
Heather (husband)
Liam
(Storm's grandfather is Callum. Storm's parents are Ian & Clarista)

Madoc (Abigail Blackmore) – Lord of Illusion
Robin (Sage Hillock) – Winter Sage
Martin
Martine (David Stone) – Sweet Mead for Lady Martine
Regina (Hunter Chase) – Ladybird
Dorothy

Echo (Garrett Blackmore) – Lady of the Mist
Edgar or Gar (different father) (Josefina Waterman) – Riding out the Storm
Eliot
Eleanor (Connor Wyland) – Dancing on Air
Elizabeth
Evan

Not related – Sorcerer Orrick (Hope Threston) – Keeper of the Flame

CHAPTER I
BLACKPOOL, ENGLAND, 1377

Thief-takers, or bounty hunters as they were sometimes called,weren't openly welcome in most establishments. Actually, they weren't welcome anywhere at all.

Hunter Chase's paid profession of bringing in fugitives to whichever lord or noble paid him the most was looked down upon in this dirty, dingy tavern on the docks. The seedy hole-in-the-wall stank from old sweat and rough sex. The soiled rushes on the floor were caked with rotten food and sticky spittle, smelling worse than the piss-filled cells of the Shrewsbury dungeon where Hunter's father had once been a guard. Rodents scurried over the patrons' feet as well as across the warped and moldy drink board where the proprietor poured whisky and strong ale to men with tattered clothes and missing teeth.

Aye, even the walls seemed to move on their own with the amount of vermin that lodged there. Still, no one inside the tavern even seemed to notice its unpleasant state. The whores sidled up to the drinking men, straddling the laps of sailors. The working girls pressed up against the drunkards while the men eagerly hiked up the tarts' skirts and fondled their nearly-naked breasts. Bawdy laughter emerged from one dark corner while a fight broke out in another. The sound of flesh smashing into flesh as well as tables over-turning, rent the air. The proprietor shouted a string of curses, flinging a throwing knife through the air. The blade lodged into the wall just next to one of the offenders' heads, nearly hitting the man. Hunter was sure blood would not only be spilled but be flowing like a river before this night was over.

No good ever came from a place like this. Hunter knew that better than anyone. The Thirsty Toad Tavern used to be where he spent more nights than he could count at one time. This rat's nest was always filled to the brim with sinners, whores, murderers and thieves.

Just the type of place he was looking for.

Hunter took a swig of ale and gently placed his tankard down atop a layer of filth on the table, being careful not to breathe too hard so as not to take on a pestilence of any kind. He bit his lip and nodded. Yes, he decided. This place was perfect.

He nursed his drink in the dark corner, patiently waiting for his target to show. Hunter had spent the last few weeks tracking down three men who not only robbed a nobleman on the road but killed one of Lord Sheffield's guards as well. Already, Hunter had managed to apprehend two of the three criminals who were now thankfully behind bars. But their leader, Guimart the Grim as the man was called, had been proving to be more than a challenge to catch. Tonight, however, Hunter's job would be finished. He had tracked the man all the way from Sheffield to the docks of Blackpool.There was no doubt in Hunter's mind that Guimart would end up here next. Especially on such a busy night. The man would want to unload the goods he'd stolen. And there was no better place to do it than amongst cutthroats and thieves.

All Hunter had to do was to clap the murderer in irons and send him back to Lord Sheffield where the thief would then be imprisoned and probably hanged. Hunter was so certain that Guimart would show up in this tavern tonight that he'd sent word to Lord Bohun in Sheffield days ago to meet him here. Two of Bohun's guards arrived earlier and now sat at the next table under hooded cloaks as well. They drank and waited for Hunter to catch and hand over the fugitive to them.

With his head down and a tankard of ale clenched in his fist, Hunter tried to remain unnoticed. If this crowd realized a man of his profession was amongst them, they'd all high-tail it out the door in the blink of an eye. Hunter needed to blend in with the patrons and at the same time keep his face and weapons hidden by his cloak so there was no chance he'd be identified. He'd spent the past few nights in here, and so far it hadn't been a problem. Still, he couldn't risk it much longer or someone would discover who he really was.

The Thirsty Toad wasn't new surroundings to Hunter. Sadly, it had been where Hunter spent many of his nights at one time when he worked as a mercenary with his father. He had a dark past that he wasn't proud of, and coming back here wasn't easy for him. But times were different now, he reminded himself. He wasn't a sword for hire anymore and didn't need to kill on command. Most of his jobs being a thief-taker involved apprehending criminals, not killing them. He only killed in self-defense now, and only if he couldn't help it.

Gone were the days of having to sell his soul to be able to feed himself. Once his father died, things had changed drastically for Hunter. Five years ago he took guardianship of his nephew, Luke, when his sister, Mary, died suddenly from a bad heart. With a child in tow, he gave up being a sword for hire. He wouldn't raise this boy the way he'd grown up. No one needed that!

Hunter took up the job of thief-taker, being able to support them both. He was also able to take the boy with him wherever he went. It wasn't the ideal situation, but it was better than being a mercenary. Plus, Hunter could keep the boy under his protection. He was doing his best to make a new life for himself and Luke. However, his thirteen-year-old nephew was quite a handful these days, and not at all easy to control. It worried Hunter that the boy might end up going down the wrong path in life.

A few more good-paying jobs like this, and hopefully Hunter's troubles would be over. He planned to find a new home in a good town to live in where nobody knew them and where he could start over. Perhaps when he stopped traveling so much, he'd find a nice town-girl to marry and settle down with as well.

He looked up to see Luke leaning against the wall near the door with his arms crossed over his chest. The boy acted as Hunter's lookout. Someone entered the establishment and Luke's body stiffened. He stood up straight, cocking his head as he perused the ugly woman who'd stepped foot in the tavern. Luke motioned to Hunter and shrugged.

Hunter smiled and downed the last of his ale. His suspicions had just paid off. Since Guimart kept evading capture, Hunter realized the man must be traveling in disguise. The Thirsty Toad only attracted one type of female in this dump, and it wasn't the ugly ones. It was the ones who came here to sell their bodies and make a quick fistful of money.

This was what he'd been waiting for and now all his efforts were about to pay off. Hunter looked over at the guards and held a finger aside his nose, giving them the signal to be ready but not to do a thing until he approached the man first. Scraping his feet slowly across the floor, Hunter prepared to stand.

Stroking the iron shackles hanging at his waist, he made sure they were still hidden by his cloak, and next to his sword that he usually wore on his back. He stood and sauntered over to the drink board where the ugly woman had already laid down a pouch. Soft whispers passed between the ugly woman and the proprietor as the guards stood and slowly followed Hunter across the room. Then the woman reached for the pouch to open it, but Hunter's hand slammed down atop it, preventing any kind of exchange.

"What have you got here?" asked Hunter, his senses on full alert as he snapped up the pouch and took a quick peek inside it.

"Let go of my things," came a deep growl. The woman looked up at him and when she did Hunter smiled at seeing stubble on her chin. Just as he thought. The *she* was a *he* after all.

"Well, Guimart, it seems your journey has come to an

end." Hunter slowly lowered his hood to reveal his identity, watching the man's eyes open wide in fright. "You're going to pay for stealing these goods as well as murdering an innocent man," Hunter continued. "You're going to prison and will probably end up on the gallows because of what you did."

Guimart spun on his heel, racing for the door just like Hunter knew he would.

"Bad move," mumbled Hunter, closing up the pouch of stolen coins and jewels and tossing it to one of Bohun's guards. "Do it, Luke," he called across the room, following the path of the fleeing man.

Luke slammed the door closed, unsheathing the sword that Hunter had given him for his last birthday. It had been Hunter's father's sword at one time. The boy held out the long blade with two hands, barely able to keep pointing the tip directly at Guimart because of the weight of the weapon and the boy's lack of muscles. Still, his action and the size of the sword made an impact on the thief. Guimart stopped in his tracks and pulled a knife. Then he changed his mind and spun around and ran in the opposite direction, heading back toward Hunter.

Hunter was skilled in using just about any weapon and had his father to thank for that. However, in this situation he could see that the sword strapped to his side wouldn't even be needed tonight. Nay, this would be even easier than he thought. He chuckled under his breath. No thief in a dress was going to be able to slip away from him.

Guimart was fast and slippery with his moves. But when he got close, Hunter's fist shot out and smashed into the man's jaw, knocking the thief to the floor.

"Enough of this," grumbled Hunter. "I've got other vermin to catch." When Guimart reached for Hunter's legs to bring him down, Hunter stomped his boot down upon the man's wrist, causing him to cry out. "If you think that hurts, wait until you see what Lord Bohun has in store for you in his dungeon." Hunkering down, Hunter quickly flipped the man onto his stomach, pulling his arms behind him and clamping the iron shackles around his wrists.

"Leave me be! I didn't do nothin,'" spat the man, fire burning in his dark angry eyes.

"We'll see about that." Hunter yanked the thief to his feet and kicked the man's knife across the floor. "Does that pouch belong to Lord Bohun?" he asked the guards.

One of the guards opened the pouch and scooped out a few of the pieces of jewelry. "Aye, this is his wife's necklace," said the guard with a nod of his head. "It's his all right. That is the thief we've been searching for."

"Aye, you've caught our man, Thief-taker," said the other. "Good job."

Hunter handed Guimart over to the guards. One of them removed a small pouch of coins that was dangling from his belt and tossed it to Hunter.

"Here's your fee, Thief-taker. Lord Bohun will be pleased with your work." The guard was not able to look Hunter in the eye when he spoke. The second guard busied himself with the thief rather than paying any attention to Hunter. Odd indeed.

Hunter took a minute to open the payment pouch and quickly glance inside. Then he jostled the small leather bag up and down in his palm weighing it. "I might be overtired and hungrier than a bear at the moment, but I assure you that I am not the fool that you must think I am. It seems to me there are a few coins missing here, boys."

Luke walked over to join him, having sheathed his sword. The boy stopped at Hunter's side, picking up the thief's knife from the floor and sticking it through his waist belt. Next, his eyes focused on the pouch in Hunter's hand.

"That is your agreed upon fee. Lord Bohun gave it to us to give to you once you completed the task," the guard said with a shrug. Everyone in the tavern became silent, waiting for another fight to break out.

"I see." Hunter stared a hole through the first man and then the other, watching them become even more nervous under his perusal. Fine then," said Hunter calmly and with a quick nod. The guards seemed to relax until they heard the rest of what Hunter had to say. "You know boys, I think I'll travel back to Sheffield with you after all."

"What? Why?" asked the guard who had given him the money. He fidgeted, not able to stand still or even look at Hunter.

"Oh, I don't know," said Hunter. "Just to make certain the fugitive gets there safely, I guess. And, of course, to thank Lord Bohun personally for my bounty as well." He jostled the pouch, making the coins clink together.

The guards exchanged worried glances with each other, seeming more than concerned now.

"Then again," said Hunter, scratching the stubble on his chin and looking toward the door. "I happened to notice that you have an extra horse with you. My nephew could use a horse of his own since we only have the one between us."

"We couldn't do that," grumbled the first guard.

"That's right. It is for transporting the prisoner," spat the guard holding on to Guimart.

"A true shame, isn't it?" Hunter shook his head. "Because, now I guess you'll have to ride double back to Sheffield, won't you?"

"Ride double? Nay, we won't do that," snapped the same guard.

"Oh, I'm afraid you will," Hunter answered with conviction. "Unless you want Lord Bohun to discover that you not only tried to cheat me by stealing part of my fee, but that in doing so, you have deceived him as well."

"They'll end up in the dungeon with the thief if Lord Bohun finds out," said Luke.

"Yes, they will," answered Hunter. "But only if they're lucky enough to escape the noose." Hunter shrugged and smiled again. "What will it be, boys?"

"Here," spat the guard who had given him the bag, handing Hunter a few coins that he had pilfered for himself from Hunter's pay and that he had kept hidden in his hand.

"That's a start," said Hunter, adding the coins to his money pouch and closing it up before tying the strings to his belt. "Luke, go ready your new mare. I'll meet you outside in a minute and then we'll leave."

"I'm getting my own horse? Really? Yes!" said Luke, slapping his hands together in excitement and turning and running for the door.

"Nay!" protested the guard. "I gave you back your coins, now leave the damned horse alone."

"Too late for that," said Hunter, following Luke. He stopped at the door and turned back around. "Oh, and don't even think of pilfering any of the goods I retrieved for Lord

Sheffield because I looked inside the pouch and know exactly what is in there. I will be contacting Bohun in a few days' time to thank him for the job. Therefore, you'd better make damned sure the prisoner gets to him along with all the stolen goods and in a timely manner."

"What if the prisoner escapes us?" asked the guard holding the man.

"Aye," said the other, catching on. "He's a thief. He might just steal the lord's jewels again and escape as well."

"None of my concern if he does because I will be contacting Lord Bohun either way," Hunter assured them. "And I warn you it'll only work against you if Bohun discovers you lost the thief and his jewels, so I wouldn't even consider trying it, boys."

"It wouldn't bode well for you either," snapped the guard.

"Is that what you think?" Hunter chuckled. "If the thief does escape, Lord Bohun will just hire me again to track him down, and my coffers will be filled a second time, so it doesn't matter to me. You see, I win either way. Now excuse me, because I need to help my nephew get situated with his new steed before we leave."

Hunter walked out to find Luke already atop the horse and waiting for him.

"Hunter, I'm ready," said Luke, calling him by his Christian name like he'd been doing more and more lately instead of calling him Uncle. "I can't believe I finally have my own horse and that we won't have to ride double anymore. This is great! I'm going to give her a strong name. Maybe I'll call her Gertrod. Nay, I want to name her Zelma."

"That's nice," mumbled Hunter mounting his horse, his

mind on anything but naming a horse at the moment. He'd never even named his horse. He just called her Mare.

"You always said we couldn't afford a second horse but now we have one just like magic.The best part is that we got her for free!"

"Aye, Luke. With two horses we'll be able to travel and track much faster now. Therefore, we'll be able to take on more work. With more work comes more money and hopefully a new home and a better life for us somewhere." Hunter headed away with Luke keeping up at his side.

"Hunter, how did you know those guards were cheating you?" asked the boy. "I didn't see you actually count the coins in the pouch. Did you?"

"Nay. I didn't."

"Then how did you know?"

"It was a risk I took and it worked in our favor." Hunter continued to ride.

"What do you mean?" asked Luke. "Are you saying you were lying?"

"I was...bluffing." Hunter didn't like being called a liar, even though that is exactly what he was.

"We gained so much from just a little lie. You sure are good at lying."

"A bluff," Hunter said once again, feeling unsettled by the boy's awe of his deplorable vice. "I was only bluffing, Luke."

"What if you had been wrong?" Luke's eyes opened wide. "What would those guards have done to you?"

"I wasn't wrong so it doesn't matter." Hunter didn't want to talk about this anymore.

"But what if you were wrong? What if they hadn't stolen

part of your fee yet you accused them of doing so." Luke continued bombarding him with his questions. "They could have killed you for that, right?"

"Nay, because I would never let that happen. Besides, I saw the way the guard couldn't make eye contact with me when he handed me my bounty. That told me all I needed to know. Plus, they were both nervous and fidgety and that was after the criminal had already been apprehended. You need to watch people's actions, Luke, to know what they are thinking. Actions always reveal the truth."

"You knew they weren't to be trusted and you were right." Luke nodded, sounding impressed. "What about the pouch of stolen goods? Did you really know exactly what was in Lord Bohun's pouch?"

"Nay. There was jewelry and coins in there but I have no idea as to how much," Hunter admitted, already regretting his answer because Luke was smiling even more.

"You lied about that too! It sounded so real that even I believed you knew."

"Bluff. I'll tell you again, I was only bluffing," Hunter said under his breath, realizing his nephew must think he was the biggest liar to walk the land. "However, those two men won't try to steal any of Lord Bohun's money or jewels now, nor will they let the prisoner escape before they return to Sheffield. I've seen to that."

"How can you be sure? Is it because they're afraid what you'll say to Lord Bohun when you contact him in a few days?"

"Mmmph," snorted Hunter, not wanting to admit that he had no plans of contacting Lord Bohun again. After all, he had his pay not to mention the man's horse now. He didn't want to give the steed back or for that matter be imprisoned for tricking the guards into letting him have the damned thing in the first place.

"I hope I grow up to be just like you someday," beamed the boy with pride.

Hunter's stomach soured at hearing this. The boy admiring him was pleasing but not for the reasons he did. "Luke, no matter if I contact Lord Sheffield or not, I had to put the fear of God in those guards, and I did. Do you understand? It was only to ensure our own well-being and safety and to seek retribution for Bohun. Plus, to make certain Guimart gets what he deserves and to make sure he doesn't escape."

"I understand," Luke answered much too quickly. Hunter had hoped the boy would at least take a moment to think about what he said. "That thief got what he deserved, the guards got what they deserved, and we got what we deserved, too. We got a horse out of the deal! All because of you."

"I'm not sure that you're understanding what I mean, son." Although Luke was only his nephew, over the past five years Hunter had started to think of him as his own son.

"I understand completely. We're better at this lying game than they are, that's all. Hunter, can you get me a crossbow and a new pair of boots next? Oh, I think I want a pet cat, too."

"Nay. Nay, I can't. You're not old enough or strong enough to handle a crossbow. Besides, you have no need for one."

"Why not? You gave me my own sword, even though I've

never had a chance to kill anyone with it yet." Luke unsheathed his sword and held it up proudly.

"That sword was my father's and you need to respect it."

"How many men do you think your father killed with this sword? I wonder how many I will kill with it someday."

Hunter's father was once a dungeon guard at Shrewsbury Castle in Shropshire. Hunter never even knew the man until one day when he was six, he found out. His mother brought him to the castle to tell his father that he existed. She was not married to the man and Hunter was naught but a bastard. Nothing ever came from the visit, nor did anything change at all. His mother was married to a different man at the time, with a daughter of their own who was Hunter's older half-sister. Hunter's stepfather never wanted someone else's bastard son and treated Hunter poorly. His stepfather had moved them away from Shrewsbury all the way to Cornwall, probably trying to escape the fact he was raising a bastard whose own father didn't even want him. By the time Hunter was thirteen, his stepfather had died and his mother then passed away shortly afterward. His older half-sister, Mary, quickly married to secure her future. That left Hunter alone to fend for himself at a young age.

All alone, he traveled back to Shrewsbury Castle to ask for his father's help. The lord of Shrewsbury wouldn't let Hunter's father raise him inside castle walls, but did grant his father the right to build a cabin in his woods. His father, Robert, did so just to be with Hunter. The man turned mercenary in order to be able to support them both. He'd given Hunter his first sword and taught him to fight. Then he took Hunter on jobs with him every time he hired out his sword. They traveled a lot and were hardly ever home. It caused Hunter to grow up fast, seeing a different world than he was used to. It hardened Hunter's heart and made him numb to people's feelings or even to the quality of life. It came from having to learn at a young age to help his father kill on command.

"No, Luke. You are not going to kill anyone," Hunter told his nephew. "That's not the life you want to live, nor what I want for you. That sword I gave you is for your protection and to be used in self-defense only. And also to help scare away thieves," snapped Hunter, not wanting the boy to end up following in his muddied footsteps.

"Well, what about my boots?" Luke picked up one foot and held it out as they rode. "I don't like these and they're getting small on me."

"When we can afford it, I'll buy you a new pair. For now, you're fine."

"Can't I get some of those expensive cordovan leather boots like the rich nobles wear?" Luke wouldn't shut up.

"Nay. Whatever for?"

"I dunno." Luke swung his foot through the air as he rode. "To kick thieves when we capture them? I want to learn to punch and fight like you do, too. Can you teach me to smash my fist into a man's face like you do to bring thieves to the ground?"

This conversation was getting worse by the minute. "There is nothing wrong with the boots you have," answered Hunter, ignoring the part about Luke wanting to fight and kill. He probably should have taught the boy how to fight by now but had been hesitant to do so. Luke had just turned thirteen. A year ago he was naught but a child. Part of Hunter wanted Luke to keep that childlike innocence as long as possible. If it wasn't already too late. The boy's life was starting to become similar to the way Hunter had grown up, and no one should ever have to live like that!

"Then if I can't get a crossbow or cordovan leather boots, how about a cat? Can I have a cat, Hunter? I've always wanted a black one so I could name her Inky. Isn't that a mysterious name? Inky." The boy's words were laced with intrigue as he smiled and stared off at the sky as he daydreamed.

"We travel too often to have a pet, so the answer is no."

"Pleeeease?" Luke was thirteen now but sometimes still acted like that eight-year-old that Hunter had first taken into his care.

"I said nay. Now don't ask again." This whole conversation was irritating Hunter and making his head hurt. All he longed for was a bit of peace and quiet.

"Well, why not?" the boy continued, not listening to Hunter's warning in the least. "You are good at getting things for free so you could do it if you wanted to. I want to learn to do that too. Teach me to bluff like you do, Hunter. Then I'll never have to work a day in my life and still have everything I've ever wanted." The boy's blue eyes lit up with excitement and it scared Hunter out of his mind. No thirteen-year-old should be so happy about the way they lived. It was not admirable at all to have to lie and basically steal just to get what they needed to survive.

Suddenly, Hunter felt no better than the thief he'd just apprehended. He thought he'd left that dark part of his past behind when he gave up being a mercenary. Now, he wasn't so sure. Being a thief-taker wasn't any better. So much for being a good influence on his nephew. Luke enjoyed getting things too easily, especially if it was by lying or cheating. That didn't sit right with Hunter at all.

A deep stab twisted in Hunter's gut and his head filled with that nagging, gnawing voice once again that he despised. It had been getting louder and louder through the years. At first he had ignored it but he couldn't do that anymore. He tried his hardest to push the voice in his head away, but it taunted him and took control of his mind. This was the voice of his dear departed sister. She'd been talking to him from the grave.

Hunter, I don't like the way you are raising my son. Luke is a good boy. You need to be a good example to him. What are you doing? What are you thinking?

"I'm doing the best I can," he mumbled under his breath, not sure Mary could hear him since she was dead. Then again, he could hear her so it probably worked both ways, he imagined.

Why does Luke even have a sword? That is so dangerous. He's too young to use it. And why are you taking him into places like that dirty disgusting tavern? With whores! He's just a boy. You are a bad influence on my baby.

"Luke is not a baby and neither is he a boy anymore. He has been forced to grow up fast with no parents. He's a young man now, Mary, even if you don't think so." Hunter spoke through gritted teeth, not liking to be controlled by a spirit from beyond. "Sister, I am trying my best to raise him. I am sorry if it isn't good enough for you. Then again, nothing I ever did was good enough for you or even Mother, was it? You all listened to my stepfather too often when he spoke badly of me."

"What did you say, Uncle Hunter?" Luke rode up next to him cocking his head and still smiling.

"Nothing, Luke. I was just thinking aloud, that's all," Hunter answered with a sigh.

Mary didn't like this lifestyle for her son and Hunter couldn't blame her in the least. He didn't care for it either, but didn't know how to change it. At least being a thief-taker was more honest of a living than being a mercenary or a damned thief. That had to count for something, didn't it? Why couldn't his sister understand that? Why wouldn't her haunting voice in his head just go away and leave him be?

Please, Hunter. Try harder. Help my son to do the right things before he is led down the wrong path forever, like you. Before it is too late to turn back and he ends up paying with his life.

Hunter's head pounded. All he wanted was to lay down and sleep for a week with a bottle of whisky gripped tightly in his fist. But he couldn't. He was responsible for the boy and had to always be on the alert. Mayhap he was going about things all wrong or could do something better. He wasn't sure anymore. But in his defense, he had never been a father before. He had no damned idea how to parent a child, let alone a restless youth who thought everything was naught but a fun game. He groaned inwardly. Why was everything in his life always so difficult? When would things start to get better? Now, in trying to help the boy and make him happy, Hunter had only gone and made the situation even worse.

CHAPTER 2
SHREWSBURY CASTLE

"Watch out, Robin," Regina Blake spoke to her brother who had been the new lord of Shrewsbury Castle for the last three years now. "I've been working with Cloud and he's learned a new skill."

Regina was not only the noble daughter of Madoc and Abbey Blake, but she'd been a falconer for many years now. Her love of birds, that she'd gotten from her father, led her to end up training falcons and hawks. She even joined the men on hunting trips and helped out to catch game with her birds of prey.

"The only thing that bird is good at is eating," scoffed Robin. "When you moved your birds here when you took up residence and I agreed, I didn't know how costly they'd be." Robin was her older and only brother. He was three years her senior, her age being twenty-one now. Regina's older sister, Martine, who married David the innkeeper, now lived at Blake Castle with their Uncle Corbett and Aunt Devon. Regina's younger sister, Dorothy, or Dot as she now liked to be called, was visiting from their parents' home in Blackmore and had been Regina's best friend her entire life.

"Robin, stop complaining," said Dot with a smile on her face. The girl was always smiling. "You should be happy that Regina moved her birds to your mews. She is the best falconer around."

"Thank you for your confidence and praise, Sister," said Regina, glad to have someone on her side. "Robin, if I must remind you, I was the one who talked Father into building a pigeon coop for you so you can now receive and send messages back and forth with your carrier pigeons like the rest of our family. You should be thanking me for moving in with you instead of complaining." She held up her left hand with her young goshawk, Cloud, perched atop the leather falconer's glove. She loved every one of her birds and cared for them as if they were her children. Cloud was the youngest and had been taking to his training so well that it made her more than pleased.

Their father, Madoc, used to raise and race carrier pigeons back when he was a thief. Before he even knew he was a noble. Because of him, all the family members, even the MacKeefes in Scotland, were able to send and receive quick messages back and forth using the talent of those little birds.

"Yes, Regina, I am grateful," Robin ground out. "However, I'm not sure Father likes the fact that your birds of prey have taken down several of his pigeons now, including one of his favorite doves."

"Don't blame my birds for that." Regina scooped a piece of raw meat out of the food bag at her side and fed it to Cloud. The goshawk eagerly gobbled it down. She'd been building trust with her newest bird by taking it with her everywhere she went and giving it lots of treats. The sun lit up the bird's colors of brown and white mottling on its back. Its cream colored underparts and the wavy bands on its tail revealed it was still a young goshawk. "If you would stop letting the pigeons out of the coop to fly when you know I am training my birds, it would stop happening."

"You are always training, it seems," remarked Robin.

"Well, that is my job," she responded.

"That's why she is so good at it," added her sister.

"Father is at the coop right now, Regina," Robin told her. "Mayhap you should put that bird away until he leaves to head back home."

"Not until after I show you Cloud's new skill." Regina looked over to the end of the open field where her apprentice, Roger stood waiting for her signal. Roger had been the apprentice of Shrewsbury's last master falconer, Cassian, who was now retired but still helped out in the mews. When Regina moved into Shrewsbury Castle with her brother and his wife, Cassian was forced to step down when she took over the position of Master Falconer. Roger continued as her apprentice instead. "All right, I'm ready, Roger," she called out, holding the bird up higher in the air. "Get ready, Cloud. This is your big chance to prove that you'll be the great hunting bird I know you will be."

Roger was near a row of hedges. He held the end of a string that had a lure attached to the end. The lure was a fake rabbit that Regina had made out of an old shoe. She'd tied real rabbit fur around it. Roger started to run and pulled the string with the lure behind him. The fake rabbit bounced over the ground after him, symbolizing a real rabbit hopping away.

"Go get it," she told her bird, sending Cloud from his perch on her arm. The bird focused on the pretend rabbit, flying with lightning speed to the lure. It dove down and clutched the lure tightly in his talons. Regina had filled the shoe with rocks for weight, so the bird couldn't lift it and fly at the same time yet. That was the first step of the training. Cloud called out to her proudly, clutching the lure and hopping with it, trying to bring the fake kill back to his master.

"Good boy," Regina called out, at the same time giving Roger a wave, happy with the way things had gone. She beamed with pride, feeling like the parent of a skilled and talented child. "Did you see that? Did you see how he caught the lure?" Regina walked across the field toward the bird. Dot and Robin followed.

"Yes, that was great," said Robin sounding perturbed and as if this didn't interest him in the least.

"Cloud will be a valuable hunting bird," agreed Dot, keeping up at Regina's side. "Mayhap someday I can learn to be a falconer too."

"Nay, Dot," growled Robin. "We need at least one woman in our family to become a real lady. You'd be better off spending your time in the ladies solar stitching instead of in the hot and smelly mews like your sister."

"Robin, how can you even say that? Dot can do whatever she pleases," scolded Regina. "Besides, being a falconer does not make me less of a lady. I think it makes me a stronger and more talented woman." She approached the bird and held out her arm, luring him back to her with another piece of meat. Cloud looked up and spread his majestic wings, releasing the lure and then flying to her, landing once again on her outstretched arm.

"Nay, our brother is right," said Dot shyly. "I do like birds, but what I enjoy even more is singing like a bird. Mayhap I'll be an entertainer someday." She stood a bit taller and prouder.

"Good for you. You do that," said Regina, running a finger over the bird's head.

"Here comes Father," announced Robin, squinting his eyes in the bright sun and gazing across the training field. "Something seems wrong."

"Children," said Madoc, approaching at a run. He held a scrap of paper in his hand. Madoc's long dark hair had begun to show signs of graying lately. Still, Regina thought of her father as one of the handsomest men she'd ever known.

"What is it, Father?" Robin ran to meet him and they conversed softly before approaching the girls. By the looks on their faces, Regina realized it was of utmost importance. And it didn't seem to be pleasant.

"Roger, please take Cloud back to the mews for now and check on the rest of the birds to make sure they have what they need." Regina handed the goshawk over to her apprentice who took the bird with a gloved hand as well. The boy was tall and skinny and about the same age as Regina.

"Yes, my lady," Roger said with a nod and did as instructed. As soon as he left, her father spoke.

"While I was caring for the flock at the coop, one of my flyers came in unexpectedly with a message.

"From where?" asked Regina.

"From home. Your mother sent it." Concern showed on Madoc's brow.

"Oh no! Is Mother all right?" asked Regina.

"She's fine," said Madoc. "Unfortunately, her note says that your grandfather has died."

"Nay. That is so sad." Dot wiped a tear from her eye. With her turned up little mouth even when the girl cried she didn't look sad but Regina knew her emotions were real.

Regina's father looked more serious than she'd ever seen him and she could tell he was deeply disturbed.

"I need to return at once to Blackmore Castle," he told her. "I'll have to make plans for your grandfather's funeral."

"Father, that means you're the new lord of Blackmore now, since Mother's father died, doesn't it?" asked Robin.

"Yes. Yes, I am," Madoc answered. "We all knew this day would come, and now there is much to do." He shook his head and looked down at the ground. "We've been expecting this for some time with his illness. Still, your mother will be devastated to have lost both her parents now."

"I think we should all go back to Blackmore at once," suggested Regina. "Mother will need our support at a time like this."

Instead of agreeing, Robin and Madoc exchanged an odd look that Regina did not understand.

"What is it?" asked Regina. "There is something you two are not telling us, isn't there?"

"Yes, I think so too. Is there something else we need to know?" asked Dot, wiping her eye with her sleeve.

"I think it is best if I go home alone," Madoc told them.

"Why?" asked Regina. "We all need to be there for Grandfather's funeral."

"Nay. Something has arisen here at Shrewsbury and it is best if Robin stays back to handle matters," said Madoc. "Besides, Sage is still feeling quite ill. It would be better if Robin doesn't leave her or ask her to travel right now."

"Sage is a healer," Dot pointed out. "She sure seems to be ill quite often lately. Can't she cure herself?"

"Not from this." Robin exchanged looks with their father once again.

"You'd better tell them, Robin. It's been too long now," said Madoc.

"Tell us what?" asked Regina.

"Oooh nooo," wailed Dot. "Is Sage about to die too?"

"Nay," said Robin, swishing his hand through the air. "We didn't want to say anything sooner because Sage is superstitious. But you might as well know that she is nearly five months pregnant. With twins, or so the midwife thinks."

"Pregnant? With twins? That is so exciting!" exclaimed Regina. "Then she swatted her brother on the arm. "Why didn't you tell us this sooner? What is the matter with you for keeping this from us? We are your sisters and need to know these things."

"I wanted to tell you, but Sage and Martine thought it best to wait until the morning sickness stage passed even though it seems to be taking forever." Robin shrugged.

"Martine knew about the pregnancy as well and yet you didn't tell us?" Regina crossed her arms over her chest and scowled. She felt left out that her brother would have told their older sister but not her and Dot. Especially since

Martine was the one whom Robin used to never get along with at all.

"Martine is pregnant, too, remember," Robin told her. "My wife needed someone to talk to who knows about these things." Robin tried to dig himself out of the hole he'd fallen into by not telling his sisters the news sooner.

"Well, we are happy for her," said Regina, flashing a smile. "Still, that is no reason to stop Dot and I from accompanying Father back home for Grandfather's funeral."

"Nay, it's not," agreed Robin. "However, that isn't quite what Father meant."

"There is no reason so important that would keep me from going home right now," stated Regina. "Mother is in need of comfort. So don't even try to stop me."

"There has been a string of burglaries lately," announced Madoc.

"Where?" asked Regina curiously, not having heard of any.

"For the past few weeks they have been happening on the road outside of Shrewsbury," Robin explained. "However, in the last few days things...important things...have gone missing from right here inside the castle walls."

"There is a thief in the castle?" asked Dot.

"Shhhh." Robin held a finger to his lips and his eyes scanned the surrounding area. "I have a feeling it might be someone who lives here. Keep this quiet for now."

"I'm sorry to hear this," said Regina. "What does any of this have to do with me or Dot?"

"None of this has to do with Dot," stated Madoc. "Actually, I think it would be nice if Dot accompanied me on my journey home, after all," he told them. "Martine is already there. So if two of my children attend the funeral, it will be sufficient."

"Wait! What about me?" asked Regina. "I don't understand why I am being forbidden to go back with you. Is it just because I live here now?"

"Nay. I've summoned someone who might be able to help us," said Madoc. "The man is a thief-taker and lives right here in Shrewsbury most of the time."

"Who is he?" asked Regina.

"His name is Hunter Chase," her father answered. "He is the son of an old friend of mine from years ago. Do you remember I told you about Robert?"

"He was a dungeon guard here at Shrewsbury before we were born, right?" asked Robin.

"Yes, that's right," answered Robin. "Plus, he knew me when I once helped out in the mews."

"Father, wasn't he also the man whose fault it was that you were imprisoned here when you were a thief?" Regina didn't understand how this man named Robert could have remained her father's friend after having turned him in and almost costing her father his life.

"I've forgiven Robert, may he rest in peace," said Madoc. The man had been dead now for some time, so Regina wasn't sure why any of this even mattered. "Regina, you are forgetting that Robert also helped to save your Uncle Garret from being executed, as well as rescued me the second time I was imprisoned." There was a lot of past history right here at Shrewsbury Castle and most of it wasn't pleasing. That was the whole reason why Regina's parents hadn't taken ownership of the castle when offered it by the king. Instead, they'd stayed in Blackmore with her mother's parents and let Robin be lord and inherit the castle instead.

"What are you trying to tell me?" asked Regina, knowing this wasn't just a conversation about memories anymore.

"Yes. About that." Madoc cleared his throat. "I would stay here and help track down the thief myself, but now I am needed back home now as you can see. However, Hunter will find the thief for us. I have complete confidence in him. He is damned good at his job."

"But?" asked Regina raising a brow. "I know there is more. Tell me how this man has anything to do with me."

"Hunter will need an alias," explained Robin. "We don't want anyone to know what he does for a living. If so, and the thief is inside the castle walls and finds out, we'll never be able to catch him. The nobles and knights are becoming quite concerned and I cannot let them down."

"What, pray tell, is this man's false identity going to be?" she asked, getting a bad feeling that she wasn't going to like their answer.

"Father thought of it, actually," said Robin, shifting his weight back and forth. "Go ahead and tell her, Father."

Madoc scowled at Robin. "Coward," mumbled Madoc from the side of his mouth.

"Someone, please tell me before I am forced to shake it out of the two of you," snapped Regina.

"Regina. Daughter." Madoc stepped forward and took her free hand in his. "You have followed in my footsteps with your love for birds, and that pleases me to no end. You not only train our hunting birds, but I've taught you to care for the flock in the coop as well."

"Robin knows how to take care of the pigeons, too," said

Regina. "And Roger is here to tend to the birds in the mews in my absence. So what is this really about?"

"Father thinks it is best if this thief-taker pretends to be working here at the castle," explained Robin. "I mean, doing something besides catching a thief."

"Good idea. Give him a job," said Regina swishing her hand through the air. "I am sure there is something you can find for a commoner to do. Perhaps he can rake out muck in the stables or wash dishes in the scullery, it doesn't matter to me."

"That's not exactly the job we had in mind," mumbled Robin.

"Then what?" she asked, not really caring what this man would do.

"Hunter is going to be your new apprentice," said Madoc with a quick flash of a smile.

"What?" Regina's eyes opened wide. "Nay." She shook her head in frustration, ripping off the falconer glove and sticking it under her arm. "Falconry takes years to learn and his presence will be temporary. I cannot and will not teach the craft to someone who doesn't even care about birds at all. It is only for those with a true passion for the art. Besides, I already have an assistant. Roger and even Cassian still helps me out. I don't need more people in the mews or the birds will become frightened." She continued her rant, not giving either of the men a chance to talk. "Besides, this Hunter man isn't a noble. Only nobles can be falconers. Everyone knows that!" Her ire was spiked and her heart raced. What kind of game was her brother and father playing? She didn't like this idea one bit.

"Don't get your feathers all ruffled, Sister," said Robin,

chuckling softly at his play on words. "It is the perfect ploy, actually. Hunter will be able to keep a better eye on everyone while he is working with you. Plus, he'll have access to the entire castle, being a noble."

"But he's not a noble!" Regina ground out.

"Nay, but everyone will think he is once you tell them so."

"And if I refuse to help?" Regina crossed her arms over her chest again and her chin jutted up in the air.

"Regina, your brother needs your help," said her father in a soft voice. "Please. I had intended on aiding him, but now that your grandfather has passed away, I am needed back home."

"I don't know." Regina pouted. "I would really like to be home to comfort Mother in her time of need instead of helping a commoner pretend he is someone that he isn't."

"One of the castle guards has had his sword stolen," Robin told her.

"I am sure he just misplaced it." Regina wasn't going to give in so easily.

"Sir Elwood's horse has gone missing, too," continued Robin. "Not to mention the brooch I gave Sage for our anniversary has mysteriously vanished into thin air."

"What?" Regina blinked several times in succession. "Sage's brooch that looks like a hawk in flight in gone? That is terrible. How could that have happened? And how can anyone lose a horse? Really, Robin! What kind of castle are you running here?"

"Now do you see why he needs your cooperation as well as the help of Hunter Chase?" asked her father. "It hasn't been easy for Robin to be accepted as the new lord of Shrewsbury."

"It's been three years now," spat Regina. "He has had plenty of time to be accepted."

"Change isn't always easy for people," said Madoc. "It seems most of the nobles and knights of Shrewsbury were hoping for a new lord that was a little...older than Robin."

"More like Father's age," said Robin, a disgusted look painting his face.

"Oh." Regina dropped her arms to her side. "I'm sorry about that, Robin. I had no idea you were having trouble being accepted here."

"It won't matter once I find the thief and imprison him. Then, I'll earn the respect I truly deserve," Robin answered.

"You mean once the thief-taker finds him," Regina corrected him.

"You know what I mean. I will be helping Hunter every minute, so it will be by my efforts as well."

"Yes. Yes, I guess you will." Regina's heart went out to her brother. He had been so proud to become lord of a castle at such a young age. Irritatingly cocky about it, actually. But by the stress showing on his face right now she could tell that it wasn't as wonderful as he had hoped it would be.

"Regina, I think Father's right. You should stay here and help Robin." Dot suddenly sided with the men. "I will comfort Mother and give her your regards. This way you can be here for Sage as well. I am sure knowing that she is going to birth twins when she already has little Martin to look after is a lot for someone who has been feeling so ill lately."

Guilt ate away at Regina. She couldn't abandon her brother

or her sister-by-marriage in their time of great need. Still, she wasn't sure she wanted to train this man named Hunter to do anything that involved her birds. She only wanted him to catch the damned thief and get out of here as soon as possible.

"Well, I..." She wasn't sure what to say.

"This robber will stop at nothing," Robin added. "Your birds are valuable and very coveted by all. They would bring in a lot of money for a thief. It would be best if you were here to keep an eye on the mews."

"What?" That took her by surprise. "Do you really think this petty thief would actually try to steal my birds?"

"He's already been bold enough to enter the castle and steal a valuable brooch. Not to mention, he was able to walk out of here with a horse without anyone noticing," Robin told her. "I don't think this thief is petty at all. He's after wealth, and lots of it. This is on a whole different scale than a bandit you meet on the road. I am sure he would not bat an eye about taking one of the most valuable things that a noble can own. A hawk or a falcon, that is."

Robin was saying all the right things to upset her and he knew it. Whether it was just to get her to agree or if he were truly concerned, it didn't matter. She couldn't—wouldn't take the risk. The last thing she wanted was for Cloud or any of her birds to be in grave danger. They were like children to her. Regina would do whatever it took to protect them.

"All right." She sighed and nodded. "I will not put my birds in danger." Regina felt as fierce as a mother bear watching over her cubs right now. "I will do what you ask, but I will not like it."

"Thank you, Regina," said Robin. The stress tainting his

face diminished. "I am sure doing the right thing will make you feel better about all of this in the end."

"The only thing that will make me feel better is to know that I am here to watch over my birds. And I promise you, while I am here, no one will get close enough to even touch them. So, let's get this thief-finder in here fast and hopefully he'll do his job and be out of here in a few days."

"Thief-taker," her father corrected her. "Although I've sent a missive by carrier pigeon to my brother, William, I am not sure if he will have had time to go to the woods to find Hunter. Being a master tailor, your uncle is very busy, you realize. Therefore, I want you and Robin to go to William's home and see if you can be of any help. You might have to track down the man yourself. I hear he's been very busy with jobs lately that cause him to travel."

"Does this man live in town?" asked Regina. "It shouldn't be hard to find him."

"Nay. He prefers the solitude of the woods," said Madoc.

"Well, what if we can't find him?" asked Regina. "Then what will you do?"

"Hopefully, luck will be on our side," answered her father. "Now go. Find him and bring him back to the castle quickly before anything else is stolen."

"Fine," Regina answered, thinking this all a fool's task and something that a page could do just as easily as she. "I will go, but I swear this man is already naught but a thorn in my side. I do not like this idea in the least."

CHAPTER 3

"Uncle William. Aunt Bernadette. So nice to see you again," said Regina trying to be polite as they entered William's tailor shop on the streets of Shrewsbury. William had been raised as a brother to her father, Madoc, even though they weren't blood related. William was thirteen years older than her father and had helped to steal Madoc and his twin sister, Echo, from Blake Castle when they were babies. Although William and his wife were kind people, Regina never fully accepted them. After all, Bernadette had been a mere handmaid and William naught but a pirate and a thief even if he had talent where sewing was concerned.

"Oh, my lady, we haven't seen you for years." Bernadette hurried over and took Regina's hands in hers.

"Aunt Bernadette, there is no need to call my sister, Lady," said Robin with a chuckle, closing the door behind them. "After all, we are family."

The shop was small but clean and tidy. There were bolts

of fabric leaning against the wall. The wooden floor was swept except for the area around the work table where William seemed to be sewing a gown. Scraps of blue silk and white lace piled up under the table where a black cat played, swatting at the pile. The place had a second floor where Regina's father had lived while growing up. William had been an apprentice to a tailor at the time named Dion. Dion had been sweet on his and Madoc's mother—their fake mother. The woman had actually been the wife of a pirate but was living a secret life.

Regina had been upstairs only once. Atop the roof was a coop with some of her father's birds. This is where Madoc had started training carrier pigeons. It eventually spread to all their relatives' homes. Coops in each of the places made it quick and easy to send messages back and forth between them. It actually came in handy and kept the family informed of trouble, visitors, and births and deaths on more than one occasion now. Regina respected her father's clever ideas as well as his skills. Madoc may have been raised as a thief, but because of her Uncle Corbett her father was now a noble, a lord and a knight.

"Robin, I suppose you are here about this missive?" William put down his sewing and picked up a small piece of parchment, carrying it across the room to them. "Madoc said he wants to hire the thief-taker?"

"Yes," answered Robin. "There have been a string of robberies at the castle lately. I cannot let it continue. I need to catch and punish the culprit. Mayhap even sentence him to death."

"I see." William looked flustered as he put the missive into a pouch at his side. Regina figured his reaction was because having been a thief most of his life, the thought of sentencing the robber to death was disturbing to him.

"Have you summoned the thief-taker yet? Where is he?" asked Regina looking around the room.

"I went to his home in the woods yesterday, but he and the boy weren't there," explained William.

"He has a son?" asked Regina in surprise.

"Nay," Bernadette interrupted. "Hunter is guardian to his thirteen-year-old nephew. He takes Luke with him on all his missions."

"A boy tracking down and bringing in dangerous cutthroats and thieves?" Regina was aghast to hear this. "What kind of a man would purposely put a child in such danger?"

"I often wondered that myself," said Bernadette. "When our two girls were young, I didn't want to let them leave my side. It is dangerous in the streets of Shrewsbury, not to mention the rest of the world."

"Yes, it is," agreed Regina, not even liking the fact she had to come to town. The streets were filled with trash and feces like most towns were. The stench from that as well as the foul scent filling the air from the tannery sickened her to her stomach. It was amazing anyone could stomach living here at all. Regina had even seen whores strutting their wares down at the tavern where drunkards were always fighting. Life within the castle walls was so different and much safer, not to mention less offensive.

"I left a note for Hunter in his cabin," William explained. "Our daughters said they saw Hunter and his nephew at the edge of the woods when they were out this morning, so I'm sure he is back by now. I would go to him myself, but I have garments to finish constructing and mending." William nodded back to his worktable where the clothes seemed to be piling up. The black cat was now atop the table inspecting the wares.

"No problem. We will go to him ourselves," said Robin heading for the door. He stopped and looked over to some cloaks hanging from nails on the wall. "Are those cloaks for nobles?"

"Yes, they are." William hurried over and picked one up to proudly show them. "I've been getting more and more work orders from nobles lately. It has taken many years but word has spread about my master skills. Now the nobles are coming to me not only for mending or alterations, but to have me design and sew new clothes for them as well."

"My husband's talent has always been admired by the nobles, ever since he the guild made him a master tailor years ago," added his wife in admiration.

"My father doesn't want anyone inside the castle walls to know Hunter's true identity," Robin said, still eyeing up the cloaks. "I'll need disguises for both Hunter and Luke. These two cloaks will work for now. Once they get to the castle, I can give them some of my clothes to wear so they'll appear to be nobles."

"You're saying you want these cloaks?" William's heart seemed to sink. "My lord, my clients will be here to pick them up any day now."

"Can't you make more for them?" asked Robin.

"You sound just like Madoc. He never respected my skills, and thought he could take and use anything he wanted," complained William. "Because of him, I almost lost my chance to become a master tailor."

"William, please. You are talking to a noble," Bernadette gently reminded him.

"We'd be more than happy to pay for the cloaks, of course." Regina stepped forward, bringing forth coins from her pouch and handing them to her uncle. "Will this do?"

William looked down at the money in his hand. "That is kind of you, Lady Regina, but this is too much." He ran his thumb over the coins, desire showing in his eyes.

"I insist," she told him. "Your work is valuable and so is your time. Please, take the money and use it to sew more cloaks for your clients."

"That is a very thoughtful gesture. We thank you and appreciate it, my dear," Bernadette thanked her. "Don't worry. William can make more cloaks before our clients arrive."

William wasn't happy about having to remake the cloaks so quickly, but the money Regina paid him did seem to ease the pain. All she wanted was to get back to the castle to watch over her birds.

"Take the cloaks and let's go, Robin," Regina told her brother, heading for the door. "I don't want to be caught in the woods or on the road once the sun starts to set."

"For heaven's sake, Regina," scoffed Robin, taking the cloaks from William. "I'm there to protect you. You don't have to worry about bandits. God's eyes, I'm a skilled knight who has fought for the king. I can handle a few bandits by myself."

"Who said it is bandits that hold my concern?" she asked, walking out the door, wondering who was going to protect her from this man they called the thief-taker.

"Hunter, I found this missive on the table." Luke ran out of the house holding a piece of parchment as Hunter tended to the horses. They had just returned from their trip to Blackpool after a long journey. All Hunter wanted to do was to sit down and relax with a bottle of whisky in his hand.

"What are you talking about?" he asked the boy, brushing down the new horse that was now his nephew's. Their cabin in the woods was tiny. It was one room and barely big enough for the two of them. Hunter had constructed it with his father when he was a boy. It wasn't in town, but then again Hunter didn't want it to be. He liked his privacy and getting away from the gossipy townsfolk. They only had an open-air structure to stable the horses, but it would have to do. The enclosure was barely big enough for the one horse and he already realized he'd have to build onto it to make it large enough for two.

"Someone was in our house when we were gone and they left this." The boy held it up to show him. Luke couldn't read, so he waited for Hunter to tell him what the note said.

"Let me see that." Hunter walked over and took the missive, realizing it was from William in town. William's brother was a noble who had once known and befriended Hunter's late father.

"What does it say?" asked Luke, stretching his neck to try to see it even though he couldn't decipher a word of it. Hunter had tried to teach the boy to read but Luke had never been interested in learning.

"It's a request for another job," he told his son, scanning

the missive quickly. "Oh. At Shrewsbury Castle," he said with a groan.

"We have a job at the castle?" asked Luke, sounding thrilled at the idea. "I can't wait to go. I want to see the knights up close. Mayhap I can even spar with them since I own a sword, too." He whipped out the sword and held it up, pretending to be fighting an imaginary knight. "I'm going to learn to kill people the way they do. I want to be the greatest warrior that ever existed."

"Put that blade away," scolded Hunter. "I told you, I gave that to you for your protection only. I don't want to hear you talking about killing anyone." He had worked with Luke in showing him how to use the sword, but the boy's strength for such a heavy weapon was still lacking. Hunter wasn't at all sure that Luke could actually use the blade to protect himself if he got into trouble. It would take a lot more work and a few more muscles before Luke was really able to wield a sword.

"Why not? You kill people," said the boy in his normally defiant manner.

Hunter felt the knot return to his stomach. True, sometimes he did accept jobs to bring back men dead as well as alive. Or, at least, he used to. Once Luke saw him kill a man, Hunter decided it wasn't what he wanted a child to every see. Since that day, he only accepted non-killing missions. "We won't be accepting this job. Now brush your horse. She is your responsibility now." He shoved the brush into the boy's hand and headed for the house.

Once inside, Hunter first removed all his weapons. Then he picked up a bottle of whisky, and read the missive once more. Shaking his head, he threw the note on the table.

Then he headed for his bed which was naught but a lumpy, dusty old pallet right on the floor. After kicking off his boots, he took a deep swig of the whisky, laying down and sinking back against the pillows. Hunter yawned and closed his eyes, finally about to get the well-needed rest he coveted more than anything right now.

A big or lengthy job like this last one always seemed to drain him. Mainly because of the energy it took. Energy not only to track down the thief but at the same time keep a sharp eye to protect his nephew and keep him from being killed. It would take days for Hunter to feel rested. He thought by giving Luke a sword it would ease his concerns. Now he realized that all it did was make his worries even worse. Luke was a handful to say the least. Hunter was getting to the point where he wasn't sure what to do with the boy anymore.

He needs someone he can look up to, came the voice of his departed sister in his head once again. This had been happening a lot lately, usually every time he desperately needed sleep. It only made him feel worse than he already did. *Mayhap being around noble knights would be good for him.*

"Go away!" he shouted, taking another long draw of whisky with his eyes still closed.

"I'd love to, but I'm afraid I can't leave without you." This was a woman's voice but not his sister's.

"Huh?" Hunter's eyes snapped open. There in the doorway to his home stood a lovely woman. For a minute, he wasn't sure if he was dreaming. She had long brown hair tied back in a braid and wore an amber gown trimmed in white lace. Her long tippets or sleeves hung to the ground. Her cloak was fur-lined and elegant and in the color of purple. She had to be a noblewoman to look like this. "Who are you? And why are you at my door?" Curiously, Hunter pushed up on one elbow.

"I am from Shrewsbury Castle," she answered. "I am looking for the thief-finder named Chase Hunter. Is that you?"

"Yes. No," he answered, still trying to figure out what was going on. He lifted the bottle and took a swig of whisky.

"Well, which is it? Yes or no?" Her face turned dark as she waited for his answer.

"First of all, it is thief-taker, not finder," he corrected her with a smack of his lips. "And you've got the rest of it backward as well."

"Backward? What do you mean, backward? You make no sense at all." She blinked several times, only managing to make her large hazel eyes seem even more alluring if that were even possible. She had to be an angel. No wench ever came to his door since he didn't have trysts when Luke was around. If Hunter needed a wench, he usually went to her. He hadn't met a woman as pleasing to the eye as this one in a long, long time now. Then again, the places he inhabited were where one would find whores and beggars, not women of her stature. There was no doubt she was a lady.

"My name is Hunter Chase, not Chase Hunter," he corrected the mix-up of her words. He swung his legs over the side of the bed, still clutching tightly to the bottle. "If you are here about the job offer, I am not interested."

"Not interested?" Her eyes narrowed to mere slits. "Why not? Are you looking to be paid more? Is that why?"

"I have no idea what the job pays but neither do I really care." Hunter never had a job offer from Shrewsbury Castle and neither did he want to go there. He wasn't allowed to live there after the death of his mother and the lord of Shrewsbury had even relieved his father of his job. No one there had liked him, even though they'd never known him. Nobles didn't treat people like him well. He didn't want to go there even for a job and be around such pompous pride. He'd probably do or say the wrong thing and end up in the dungeon with his luck. "Please leave. I'm busy."

"I can see that." Her eyes settled on the bottle in his hand. "How about tomorrow when that whisky is all gone and you need money to buy more? Will you be free then? *Thief-taker?*"she stressed his title in a mocking tone. Then she boldly walked over to the side of his bed, standing there staring down at him with her hands on her hips making him feel like a scolded child.

Hunter didn't like the fact that the woman was insinuating he was a drunkard when she didn't even know the first thing about him. Neither did he appreciate the way she looked down her nose at him as if he were not as good or worthy as she. He didn't have a lot of money and he might not be a noble, but he still had his pride. He'd be damned before he let her take that from him too because it was all he had left. He put the bottle down on the floor and slowly stood, towering over her.

"My, you are a tall one." She slowly uncrossed her arms, letting them fall to her sides. "And your chest and shoulders are so...wide." Her eyes trailed upward, meeting his gaze. He would have liked to think she was perusing him in a sexual manner the way most women did, but this wench showed no pleasure in her gaze and held disdain only. The fresh spring breeze drifted in from his open door, bringing her scent of rosewater and cinnamon with it. It assaulted his senses, even if it was in a pleasing manner. Her skin wasn't as white as most nobles, telling him she was no stranger to the sun and it made him wonder why. Was it by accident or by choice? A rather ruddy tone stained her cheeks, making her seem as if she were blushing. Her turned-up little nose and turned-down pouty mouth made her look sultry, even for a rigid noblewoman.

"What did you say your name was?" he asked, feeling the need to know more about her. He didn't know anyone from Shrewsbury Castle since he hadn't stepped foot inside those walls since he was thirteen and seeking his father. Once his father left to become a mercenary, even his father's old friends inside the castle walls wouldn't have anything to do with him again. Hunter was sure he had never seen this woman before.

"I didn't say," she replied.

"Then tell me."

"Why do you want to know?"

The girl was feisty and he chuckled inwardly, wondering what kind of game she played. If she was going to invade his home and privacy and make him feel violated and uncomfortable and not even tell him her name, then she had a lot to learn. Right now, all he wanted was for her to feel the same way as he.

Without waiting for her to say another word, he decided to teach the wench a valuable lesson. He reached out and pulled her into his arms and pressed his mouth up against hers in a big kiss.

He had thought that would be enough to make her turn and run out the door with her tail between her legs. Once again, she surprised him. She oddly didn't try to get away from him. Nay, she didn't even push him or stomp on his foot or try to knee him in the groin which was what he highly expected from her. The kiss lingered, and with it grew his curiosity about this intriguing stranger. Her lips tasted like honey. The curves of her breasts pushed up against his chest, quickly reminding him that he hadn't had a wench in his bed in a long time now. Lust grew within him. He daringly let his hands slip lower, not able to stop himself from cupping her pear-shaped backside. Pulling her even closer, he gave her delectable rounded cheeks a quick squeeze. Hunter's manhood stirred. Damn, was this really happening?

"What the hell are you doing?" shouted a man. "Release my sister at once!"

Hunter dropped his arms to his sides in surprise and quickly stepped away from the girl. A nobleman stood in his doorway with his sword raised high above his head. Before Hunter could even say a word, the girl stepped forward. Her hand shot out and she slapped him hard across the face.

"Ow!" he said, his hand going to his bearded cheek, still able to feel the sharp sting even through all that hair. "What was that for?"

"It was for thinking you had the right to even touch a noblewoman let alone kiss one!" Fury showed in the girl's eyes along with a tinge of embarrassment if he wasn't mistaken. Below the surface of her big sparkling hazel orbs, he was sure he saw a scant tinge of...pleasure, too. Hunter had made a living out of reading people. This woman, noble or not, was no exception. Nay, this girl didn't despise him as much as she was trying to make her brother believe.

"I am not armed and neither am I trying to hurt the wench." Hunter raised his hands in the air. "Please. Put down your blade."

"It's all right, Robin. It's the truth," said the girl in a voice that sounded much too sultry to Hunter's ears.

The man named Robin scanned the room, his eyes settling on Hunter's weapons atop the table. Then his eyes darted back to Hunter and slowly he lowered and sheathed his sword. "Well, all right. If you're sure."

"In my defense, since you wouldn't tell me your name, I had no idea you were noble," he bluffed, hoping they would believe it. "My lady," Hunter added with a smile, bowing to her as was proper.

"Regina, I told you to wait for me before you entered the house," scolded Robin as he made his way over to them.

"Regina. That's a pretty name." Hunter raised a brow. "Although, I must admit I expected more of a warrior name by the way you hit." He rubbed his jaw to make his point. "Mayhap Ursula or Eydis, or mayhap even Thomasina," he said with a small chuckle.

"I am Lord Robin Blake of Shrewsbury Castle and this is my sister, Lady Regina," said the nobleman. He reached out and rested one hand on his sister's shoulder. The other remained on the hilt of the sword at his side. "Are you the thief-taker named Hunter Chase that my father mentioned?"

"I am he, my lord," said Hunter bowing to Robin this time. "I beg your forgiveness for my inappropriate behavior with your sister. However, when a woman comes to my door in the woods unescorted, you have to realize that the last thing I think is that she is noble."

"Nay, it's not your fault." Robin glared at his sister. "Regina cannot seem to follow a simple instruction."

"Robin, don't waste your time here," said the girl with her nose in the air again. "This man has already refused the job, so it is time we return to the castle and look elsewhere."

"Really? You refused to help me?" asked Robin. "My father, Lord Madoc Blake said he was friends with you father at one time and was sure you would take the job."

"Ah, yes, Madoc." Hunter chuckled, remembering now why the name seemed so familiar. His father had told him all about the thief who became a noble. And William, the tailor in town was all part of this crazy story too. Still, his father always spoke highly of Madoc. "My lord, I think your sister is confused about what I said."

"I am not!" she spat. "You told me to my face that you wouldn't take the job."

Hunter raised a finger in the air. "That's not exactly true. I believe my actual words were that I was not interested. However, I might be persuaded to hold interest in your request after all."

"So, what does that mean? You'll take the job then?" asked Robin. "We haven't even discussed your fee yet. How much do you want?"

"That depends." His eyes settled on Regina again. "I don't know any of thedetails yet. So mayhap one of you can tell me what will be required of me?"

"Of course we can. There have been a string of burglaries lately at the castle," explained Robin. "My father and I believe the thief might be someone who lives inside the castle's walls."

"And you want me to catch him," said Hunter with a nod.

"You'd be living at the castle and your identity would be hidden during this time so as not to alert the thief," Robin continued.

"A fake identity? Who would you make the others believe that I am?" The only way he'd even step foot inside the walls of Shrewsbury again would be in disguise. He didn't want to be around so many nobles knowing he was a commoner. A mere thief-taker. Plus, there was always the chance someone there might recognize him as Robert's grown son.

"You'll be the falconer's new assistant," said Robin, almost making Hunter laugh aloud.

"Falconry?" Hunter crossed his arms over his chest and made a face. "I'm not sure about that. You see, all I know about birds is how to kill and eat them for dinner."

"Nay! You won't be killing any of my birds," ground out the woman.

"*Your* birds?" Hunter's curiosity was really piqued now.

"Yes. My sister is our falconer," explained Robin.

"Master Falconer," Regina so smugly reminded her brother.

"Yes, Master Falconer," said Robin, glancing at his sister and then returning his attention to Hunter. "You'll be disguised as a noble and working with her in the mews."

"Really." He perused the woman once again, liking the idea of working side by side with such an intriguing and feisty beautiful woman. Especially since he discovered the way she kissed a stranger held so much passion. That only made him wonder what else she could do. Or what she might be willing to do. "I'm...not sure." Perhaps sidling up with a noblewoman wasn't a good idea. It would most likely only cause him trouble.

Hunter's answer seemed to surprise Regina. Her head snapped upwards.

"Not sure?" she asked. "What is there not to be sure about? You will be living the life of a noble, eating the best foods and sleeping in a bed instead of on a dirty pallet on the cold floor." Her eyes roamed back to his pathetic sleeping arrangements. "How could a commoner say no to that? It is a chance of a lifetime for someone like you."

Chance of a lifetime indeed. Hunter was tempted but at the same time disturbed by how he was being treated. "I have a nephew who I am sure you've already met outside," said Hunter. "I am his guardian and won't leave him while I live at the castle. Luke goes on every job with me."

"Yes, we've heard," said Robin. "That is why we brought two cloaks with us. Your nephew is welcome to join you."

"He is?" Hunter didn't expect this at all.

Just then, Luke walked in the door wearing a long cloak lined in ermine. It was too big for him and dragged on the ground behind him in the dirt. He held his sword in his hand and raised it up, getting it caught on the cloak until he shook it loose.

"Look, Hunter," said the boy. "I have a cloak like a noble now. Things just keep getting better and better. Now when I kill someone with my sword, I will be just like the knights of the castle."

"The boy calls you Hunter instead of Uncle?" asked Regina as if she didn't approve of the fact. It was scary how her voice raining down disapproval on him sounded so similar to Mary's voice in his head, coming to him from the grave. "My, he sounds bloodthirsty too."

Accepting this job went against everything Hunter believed to be good for the boy. How could he expose poor Luke to so many haughty nobles? They would never fit in, not even wearing a disguise and he knew it. It would be like selling his soul to the devil to put himself and Luke through this. Hunter wanted to say no, but something made him nod in agreement. Perhaps it was because of the way the wench looked at him and her condescending tone. Aye, it was only to rile her since he knew she didn't really want him at the castle at all and he knew it. If he was going to be uncomfortable then by all means, she should she. "All right. We'll take the job," he said, noticing a small fuzzy feather clinging to the girl's hair. He reached out and picked it up with two fingers and held it out to her. "A feather from your pillow perhaps? Spending too much time in the bedchamber?"

"Nay. It is from my birds," she snapped. She slapped his hand away and scowled at him through narrowed eyes.

"I am at your service, my Lady Falconer," he told her with an amused chuckle. Aye. This was going to prove to be even more entertaining than anything he had ever done in his life.

CHAPTER 4

By the time the traveling party got to the castle it was already sunset and the day was just about over. Hunter felt all the eyes on him as they rode through the gates into the courtyard. Sitting atop his horse dressed in the cloak of a noble, he felt like such a fake. A big liar. He glanced over at Luke. The boy was smiling from ear to ear, enjoying every minute of this immensely. That concerned Hunter.

Robin dismounted quickly and immediately two stable workers ran over to him. One was old and the other young.

"We'll take the horses, my lord," said the boy who seemed to be about Luke's age. The older man with him eyed up Hunter suspiciously.

"You have guests, my lord?" asked the man as Robin helped his sister dismount.

"We do," Regina answered for him. "Please take their horses for them." Even though this was her brother's castle,

Lady Regina wasn't afraid to give orders as she saw fit. She was nothing like a normal lady who would be silent and seen but rarely ever heard. Robin glared at his sister but didn't reprimand her in front of everyone. It made Hunter wonder if he refrained himself out of respect for his sister or because he was afraid of the wench. That amused him more than anything.

"Nay!" protested Luke when the boy tried to take the reins of his horse. Luke had dismounted and grabbed the reins back. "No one is going to take my horse since I just got her." Luke looked over to Hunter for help. "Right, Hunter?"

"Hunter?" The older man cocked his head. "That name and your face are familiar. Don't I know you from somewhere?"

"Nay, you don't, Alfred," said Regina much too quickly. "These are nobles from...from afar."

"Really." Alfred took the reins of Regina's horse. "I could have sworn I've seen him somewhere. Mayhap in town."

Hunter realized the man must know him from his job of being a thief-taker. After all, the last time Hunter was here he was not more than a child and now he was an adult. This man, being a groom, probably traveled to town often. Hunter decided he had better say something quickly to remedy the situation. His nephew already ruined his alias by calling him Hunter aloud.There was no sense in hiding his real name now.

"I'm sure you might have seen me around," Hunter told the old groom as he got off his horse.

"What are you doing?" whispered Regina, scowling at him, obviously wanting him to keep his mouth closed.

"So, we have met before, my lord?" asked Alfred. "When and where?"

"Alfred, people call me...Lord Hunter. My name is Hunter Blake. He decided at the last minute not to use his real surname."This is my nephew, Luke." He shot Luke a look to stay quiet, having told him earlier that they couldn't reveal to anyone who they really were.

"Hunter Blake," repeated Alfred with a hand to his chin. "Then you are related to Lady Regina and Lord Robin?"

"Well, actually he's not—" Regina started speaking but Hunter cut her off.

"Yes, I am. However, I'm not closely related. I am a distant...cousin. On their mother's side."

"What?" squeaked Regina, looking horrified at the story he was concocting.

"Her mother's side?" Alfred scratched his head. "And yet you use the surname of Blake, my lord? I don't understand."

Damn, he hadn't thought things through clearly because he was still too tired from his last mission. "Yes," he said, clearing his throat, hoping to hell he could come up with a tolerable excuse. He hated the fact that once again in front of his nephew he was lying. "It was because their mother's sister, yes that's it, she married their father's half-brother. From his second marriage. It's complicated."

"I'll say," mumbled Robin under his breath.

"Do you remember me at all, Lord Hunter?" asked Alfred.

Hunter's heart sped up. The man was testing him and no one could come to his rescue now. "I'm sorry, I don't," he answered, hoping this would be the end of the conversation.

Hunter noticed that the younger stableboy seemed to be about thirteen or fourteen years old, a bit older than Luke. His guess was that the boy was born here because he seemed very familiar with the job and stables. "Is this your grandson?"

"Yes. How did you know?" asked Alfred.

"A lucky guess. What is your name?" Hunter asked the boy.

"My name is Alfred," answered the child.

"An excellent name." Hunter looked back at the old man.

"You can call me Al and my grandson, Fred," the older man suggested. Everyone around here does. It avoids confusion."

"Well then, Fred. Would you be kind enough to care for my horse for me?" Hunter spoke to the boy.

"Why do you have your sword strapped to your back?" asked Fred, taking the reins from him. "Are you a knight?"

Damn, Hunter forgot about that. Only warriors and bounty hunters wore swords in this manner. He was in such a hurry to leave that he had just slipped the cloak right over his shoulders and over the sword as well.

"You could say I'm a fighting man, yes," he answered.

"I'm a fighting man, too. See my sword?" Luke reached for his sword. Hunter's hand shot out to stop him.

"My nephew, Luke, always says he wants to be a knight someday," Hunter told them with a chuckle, trying his best not to lie but also not to be too direct with his answers.

"My lord, the cooks are waiting to serve the meal." The castle's steward rushed out of the keep to speak with Robin.

"Yes, thank you, John. We will be right there. Follow me, Lord Hunter," said Robin.

They all walked to the great hall and Hunter stopped just inside the door. The room was noisy and crowded. Long trestle tables lined the walls and continued down the middle of the room. Each of them were filled with people. Some looked like nobles, some knights, and others were dressed more like commoners. There was a table near the back of the hall where some of the servants seemed to gather. Cupbearers and kitchen maids rushed back and forth with pitchers of ale and large empty platters. They seemed to be waiting to serve the meal. Most likely as soon as the nobles sat down. Wine flowed freely and music from the gallery filled the air. There was a jester walking around juggling eggs in the air. Children followed him, jumping up trying to catch the eggs. Several dogs hid under the tables waiting for scraps of food.

"You'll eat up here with us at the dais," Regina told him, leading him to a trestle table that was raised on a platform at the front of the room. Already a good dozen nobles sat there waiting. There were a few empty chairs in the middle of the table. It was all very overwhelming to be here at all.

"Down here is fine," he told her.

"Nay, nobles eat at the dais. It is mostly only commoners who eat below the salt," she told him. "Take a seat at the dais."

"Nay." Hunter shook his head. "I don't think so." The last place he wanted to be was on display for the entire castle.

"Why not?" she demanded to know. She leaned closer and spoke softly. "Have you forgotten that you are supposed to be a noble. If you were truly my cousin you'd be sitting with me."

"It's too much of a risk that someone might recognize me if I am up there on display."

"I thought you didn't have much contact with the townsfolk," said Robin, having overheard their conversation. "That's what William told me."

"If you travel all the time, plus the fact you live like a hermit in the forest, it is possible that no one will even know you here," added Regina. "You are at the castle now. This life is much different from that of your little hut in the woods."

"Well, I want to eat up at the dais," said Luke, his eyes widening.

"Only adults," stated Robin. "However, you are welcome to sit with the children of the nobles over there." Robin pointed across the room where a horde of children couldn't seem to sit still.

"I think it would be better if Luke and I ate in our chamber," suggested Hunter, not trusting that Luke could keep his mouth shut around all those children. "Can you just direct us to where we'll be staying, please?"

"Of course, but are you sure that's what you really want to do?" Regina's eyes begged him to stay. She leaned over and spoke softly once again. "I thought being amongst the people would make it easier for you to identify the thief."

"Yes, but not tonight," he protested. "We just returned from a long trip and my nephew needs his rest."

"I am a little tired," admitted Luke, stifling a yawn with his hand.

"Fine, then. I can have my steward show you to your chamber and a page will bring food and drink to your room," Robin offered.

"Thank you." Hunter nodded, his head still pounding like a drum in his ears.

It wasn't ten minutes later and Hunter and Luke were sitting in a bedchamber that was bigger than their cabin and horse stall put together. They ate food so delicious that he thought he'd died and gone to heaven. There was a full flagon of red wine that the page brought, and it tasted richer than any wine he'd ever had. A platter of sweetmeats was nearly empty since Luke decided he liked the candied fruit better than the quail or the dubious-looking meat that he couldn't identify.

"Hunter," said the boy, yawning again. "I think I'm going to like living here at the castle." He put down his cup and his eyes started to close.

"Aye, well, don't get too used to it, Luke. We won't be staying long."

"Where do I sleep?" asked the boy, standing up and stretching.

"Well, considering there is only one bed but it is big enough for four, I'd say we'll share its comfort." He pointed to the bed that was up two small stairs and surrounded by long velvet bedcurtains hanging from irons.

"What are the curtains for?" asked Luke stripping down to his braies and pulling back the covers and climbing into bed.

"I guess for privacy." Hunter downed the rest of his wine after first using a hand cloth provided to wipe the grease of the meal from his fingers. He'd have to ask Regina tomorrow just what the food was that he'd devoured. Whatever it was, it tasted much better than the pottage he often made or even the hare he usually hunted and killed for their meals.

"Although, I'm not sure why anyone would need that much privacy," he finished telling Luke. Hunter started thinking about Regina again. He thought of the way she looked with those womanly curves. Her delicate yet alluring scent seemed to be stuck in his nose and it was driving him crazy. Then there was that kiss they shared. The way she'd kissed with so much passion had his mind racing and his senses reeling. All he could think of was what he'd like to do with her atop a big luxurious bed like this, and behind those lush, closed velvet curtains.

He sprang to his feet, shaking the lustful thoughts from his head. When he noticed Luke was already sleeping, he decided to go for a walk in the night air to clear his mind and cool his hot, aching loins. Mayhap a dip in the cold lake would cure his problems. What was wrong with him? Someone like him should never even be entertaining ideas about taking a noblewoman to his bed. He never should have kissed her either. Now, she'd ruined everything. No other wench would ever suffice again. He'd always be comparing his latest tryst to Lady Regina. Hell, he had enough trouble in his life and didn't need to be locked behind bars for seducing someone of such a high status.

He closed the door to the room softly, hurriedly making his way down the stairs. Cheery music rent the air. Hunter stopped just outside the door to the great hall, seeing people laughing and drinking and eating more food than he'd ever seen in his life. There were strolling minstrels playing music and a few of the men already well in their cups, pulled women up from the table to dance with them.

His eyes roamed over to the dais. He had hoped to see Regina, but was disappointed to find that she was not there.

Robin sat with a woman who had a round face and strawberry-blonde hair. She was probably his wife, he decided. Some of his knights and ladies of the castle looked toward the entrance, causing Hunter to quickly step back into the shadows. He did not want to be seen. Regina's seat next to Robin's was empty so there was no need to tarry here any longer. It was probably a good thing she'd already left because seeing her right now would only make him want to kiss her once again. And that wouldn't do a damned thing to relieve him of his little problem.

He turned and headed out of the hall and made his way down to the castle courtyard. The sun was just setting and it lit up the horizon with a beautiful glow of reds and oranges, bringing the sky to life. The castle was large with an inner and outer bailey. He'd noticed an orchard when he'd arrived, right inside the castle walls. There were many out-dwellings such as the forge, the stables, the barracks for the soldiers and, of course, the mews. Wanting to be alone to think, he decided to get his horse and take a ride outside the castle walls to a lake he'd noticed not far from the drawbridge.

Approaching the lake, which appeared surrounded by brush, he realized it was a perfect place to go to be alone. The sunset only got better and the water looked inviting. There was no one around so he tied the reins of his horse to a tree and decided to go for a quick swim to cool down.

After kicking off his boots, he removed his tunic. He was about to remove his breeches when the sound of a hawk crying out caught his attention and made him look up at the sky.

There, silhouetted on the glow of the horizon, was a bird of prey with wings spread majestically as it seemed to float gracefully through the air. It was a hawk or falcon of some sort. He wasn't sure which. He watched the bird it as it got closer, realizing it was preparing to land. It also seemed to have leather ties dangling from its feet. He knew at once it was one of the birds from the castle mews. Hunter headed down to the shore in his bare feet, peering around the brush. That's when he saw her.

Regina stood on the shore with a golden glow from the sky lighting up her smiling face. Her hand was in the air and on it was a falconer's glove. She stretched her arm upward toward the heavens as if she were summoning the wind itself and gave a sharp whistle. The bird flew to her obediently and landed gently on her gloved hand. Regina praised the bird with soft, gentle words and quickly gave it a reward from her pouch.

"You are such a good bird, Lightning," she said, stroking the falcon on the head.

Fascinated by her expertise in handling the bird, Hunter made his presence known.

"I am surprised you are not with the nobles eating in the great hall, my lady." He walked toward her. "Instead, I find you outside the castle walls, alone and with a hawk."

Startled, Regina spun around too quickly. The fast motion startled her bird and caused it to take off again in flight.

"You frightened Lightning," she scolded. "And he is a peregrine falcon, not a hawk."

"Sorry." He shrugged. "They all look the same to me."

"What are you doing here, Hunter?" Regina's heart raced. She had left the great hall early not only to let Lightning fly in the sunset but because she needed to get away and think about what happened earlier that day in the thief-taker's cabin. The man had been bold enough to not only touch her but to kiss her. She had all but melted in his arms, not able to move away.

"I could ask you the same thing, my lady. Do you usually skip a meal just to fly a bird?"

"Don't make it sound like such a menial task when it is more important than eating. Lightning loves the sunsets. He deserves to fly more than he usually gets to do. It is not normal nor healthy for any bird to be tethered to a perch for so long. I like to let my birds feel freedom as often as they can."

"They are hunting birds, my lady, and are expected to be tied to their perches when not working." Hunter stopped right next to her, so close that she swore she could feel his body heat radiating out and touching her from that gorgeous bare chest he didn't even try to cover in her presence. "They have a job to do and like most of us they will never know what it is to truly be free."

His words sounded so sad but at the same time didn't seem bitter. To her, his tone came across as almost serene. It was as if he'd made peace with the idea of being naught but a simple commoner for his entire life. She got the feeling he wasn't the kind of man who ever strived to spread his wings and soar to new heights. He seemed cautious and not willing to take risks. Then again, he was a thief-taker and she knew risk must be involved with a job like that, so mayhap she just didn't understand him.

"Watch out," she told him, dipping her free hand into

the bag at her side. "Lightning doesn't like to be crowded when she lands."

"Sorry." He took a step back.

With her left hand in the air, she stood still. The bird landed with stealth atop her glove and she fed it a scrap of meat once again.

"The bird seems devoted to you."

"She should. I am the hand that feeds her. She will do anything I want." Once she said it, she realized that it might have sounded haughty. After all, she had fed Hunter tonight as well.

"How old is she?" he asked, once again taking a step closer.

"Lightning is five," she told him, wrapping the jesses, leather strips attached to the bird's legs, around her hand. "However, my oldest bird, Hera, is a gyrfalcon and I've had her the longest. She is eight now."

"I don't think I'll ever be able to tell one bird apart from another."

"You will in time. However, you haven't even met them all yet. When you do, you will see the difference."

He shook his head. "I really don't think I'll ever be able to do what you do. Was it hard to learn the skills of being a falconer?"

"It comes with time and a lot of hard work. And no, you will never be able to do what I do, you are right." She gave Lightning another scrap of meat.

"Thanks for having so much faith in me," he said leaning in closer to peruse the bird. He reached out to touch it but the bird squawked and opened its beak, letting out a rapid kak-kak-kak sound that startled

Hunter. He quickly pulled back his hand. "Why did she do that?"

"Lightning is cautious since she doesn't know you. Or like you," she added under her breath, reaching out to gently stroke the bird's back.

"How can you say the bird doesn't like me?" Hunter scowled. "She's probably just being territorial, that's all."

"Nay," she answered. "Her territorial call is kee-kee-kee. You definitely made a bad first impression."

"I give up," mumbled Hunter. "How am I supposed to be a falconer's assistant if the bird won't let me near her?"

"You have to earn the bird's trust first." Regina looked over at him and directly into his eyes. "Just like with a woman," she said in a mere whisper.

"I see." Hunter found himself being drawn into Regina's big, beautiful eyes. With the setting sun reflecting in her hazel orbs he saw small specks of green and even orange bringing them to life. "And how long does it take to gain that type of trust?" It took all his control not to reach out and cup her cheek or push back a stray strand of her hair behind her ear. But after that slap he received, he decided he'd better take things slow. Besides, if he tried to touch her, the damned bird would probably attack and sink its sharp beak into his flesh.

"It takes longer than you think," was her answer.

"Do you mean...for the bird...or for a woman?" he asked in a deep voice, wanting her to trust him the way her bird trusted her. He longed for Regina to welcome him and fall into his open arms. He fantasized of her resting her head against his chest as he stroked her soft hair the same way she stroked the bird's feathers.

With their gazes interlocked, the intimate moment lingered. Her stare was strong and brave. Surprisingly, she did nothing to break the connection between them. There was a curious nature locked deep within her eyes that called to him. Hunter found himself wondering if she was as intrigued by him as he was her.

"Where are you clothes?" she asked, nearly choking on the words, or so it seemed. Her gaze slowly lowered from his eyes to his bare chest.

"I was planning on taking a quick dip in the lake. Then I saw you."

"A dip in the lake? Whatever for?"

He squirmed a little and then nonchalantly crossed his arms over his groin. The last thing he wanted was for her to notice the bulge growing under the fabric of his breeches.

When Regina's eyes traveled lower, she almost gasped aloud by what she saw and quickly looked the other way. This man was filled with lust. The bulge in his breeches proved it. She shouldn't be here alone with a lusty half-naked man when it was soon to be dark. Not to mention, she was with a stranger she barely knew and also unescorted. Regina didn't know anything about this man at all. She wasn't even sure she could trust him.

"I was hot," he said, making her skin warm just hearing his words. Did that bulge in his breeches have anything to do with her? Deep down she rather hoped so. "I wanted to cleanse myself from the dust and dirt of my last trip."

"Nobles do not bathe in the lake," she told him, feeding more to her bird, trying her hardest not to look at him anymore. The more she did, the more she wanted him to kiss her like he did at the cabin. "If you want a bath, tell the steward. He will have servants bring up a wooden tub which they will fill with hot water."

"Really? Where? To my bedchamber?"

"Of course. Where else?"

"I have never bathed indoors before."

She glanced at him from the corner of her eye and shook her head. "Then you'd better start. If you want anyone to believe for a moment that you are a noble, you had best act the part. That goes for your nephew, too."

"Have no fear, I can do it, my lady. However, I am not so sure about Luke."

"What do you mean?" She turned to look at him and instantly regretted it. His nipples were hard. Hopefully just from the cool night breeze. His chest was so wide and sturdy and his arms bulged with muscles. There was a small smattering of dark hair trailing down his chest and disappearing into the top of his breeches. The hair on his head was brown and hung down to his shoulders. He had a beard and mustache covering his face and craggy thick brows. His features were very handsome for such a rugged and unrefined man. Hunter stood much taller than most of the men at the castle. He still towered over her now, and he had bare feet.

"I have been having a hard time raising the boy," he explained. "Luke doesn't seem to want to listen to a word I say."

"How old is he?"

"He recently turned thirteen."

"That's why. It is only going to get worse before it gets better. I know for a fact since that is how my brother Robin was at that age." She walked over and sat down on a rock, removing a small leather hood from her side pouch and slipping it over the bird's head and eyes. The falcon's beak stuck out through the opening.

"What is that for?" Hunter still kept his distance.

"Birds of prey are easily distracted and startled," she told him. "Having a hood over their eyes helps to calm them. You can come closer now, it's all right."

"Thank you," he said, walking up next to her.

"What about the boy's parents?" she asked. "Can't they do something to control him?"

"Nay. They are both dead and I am his guardian now."

"I am sorry. How long has it been?"

"I have been raising Luke on my own for the last five years. Right after my sister, Mary, passed away."

"Do you have any more sisters? Or what about brothers?"

"Nay. It's just me now. Mary was a half-sister, actually. She was a few years older than me."

"How old are you?"

"I am twenty-nine, my lady. How old are you?"

Her head snapped upward. "I am not certain it is proper to ask a noblewoman her age, but if you must know I am twenty-one. Hunter, I am curious. Do you have any children of your own?"

"I would think that was an obvious no since I can't seem to handle the boy I have taken guardianship over."

"Then, you've never been married?"

"You certainly do ask a lot of personal questions."

"If you are going to be living within the castle walls and working with me every day it is important that I know all about you."

"Ah. I see. So you can...trust me?" He flashed her a smile.

"I am not sure that will ever happen," she mumbled, turning to pay attention to her bird.

"No," he said.

"No, what?"

"No, I haven't been married. My life hasn't been all that easy, you see."

"What does that mean?" She turned back to look at him once again, seeing the turmoil in his eyes.

"My mother died when I was thirteen. My father raised me until he died when I was twenty. Then I was on my own until five years ago when my sister died too. That is when I took Luke to live with me."

"I'm sorry for all your hardships."

"Thank you. It is a part of life, I guess."

"Was your family free? Or were you serfs?"

"Neither. My mother and stepfather were farmers. They owned a small plot of land that produced our food."

"Stepfather? What about your real father? The one who knew my father?"

"That...doesn't matter."

"My father said he once worked right here at Shrewsbury Castle. As a dungeon guard, I believe."

"Yes. That's correct. He was a guard here before he left Shrewsbury Castle to raise me."

"Why did he leave?"

"If you must know, it is because the lord of the castle at

that time refused to let him raise his bastard son at the castle. We were shunned by all. My father wasn't able to keep his job and raise me both."

"I'm sorry. So what type of job did he have after he left the castle?" She could tell all her questions were disturbing him greatly, but she wasn't exactly sure why.

He turned and looked out over the water. "Excuse me, my lady, but I need to get back to my chamber in case Luke awakes. I don't want him wandering about a strange castle on his own."

"All right. I understand." She stood with the bird still on her arm. "Report to the mews in the morning just after sunup."

"Sunup? That early?" He seemed surprised.

"I start training early in the day. Before it gets too busy around the castle. It only distracts the birds."

"All right. First thing in the morning then, my lady." He started to walk away as the sun disappeared on the horizon.

Regina couldn't look away as she watched his half-naked form moving smoothly and graceful over the land as he made his way to the water. She called out after him. "Did you want me to have the servants bring you a bath?"

He stopped and turned back to look at her from down by the lake.

"No need, my lady. The lake will be fine." With that, he turned his back to her and dropped his breeches as well as his braies. He stood at the edge of the lake stark naked. She gasped, almost startling Lightning again when she jerked backward and almost fell. Then she saw him dive into the lake making a big splash as his naked back end disappeared under the water.

Regina turned and walked back to her horse at a near run. Mayhap she had been severely mistaken when she thought Hunter Chase was not a risk-taker at all. His actions tonight told her that he was not only a risk-taker but also a very dangerous man to be around.

Unfortunately, one thing that attracted Regina like a moth to a flame was a handsome, sexy, unpredictable and dangerous man. That is, a man just like Hunter Chase.

CHAPTER 5

Hunter had overslept the next morning, being so tired from the day before.Therefore, he was late getting to the mews with Luke. The spring air was chilly this morning. The sun was bright and there were little to no clouds in the sky. Aye, the day was promising to be beautiful, just like Lady Regina.

"Why can't we have something to eat before we start working? I'm hungry," complained Luke, not wanting to go to the mews with Hunter. The boy was more intrigued by what went on inside the castle. When they had passed by the kitchen on their way out to the courtyard, the aroma of fresh bread and what smelled like bacon made Hunter's stomach growl as well.

"We have a job to do," Hunter reminded his nephew. "I promised Lady Regina we'd be at the mews first thing in the morning and I've already let her down."

"I would rather explore the castle than go watch stupid birds all day," spat Luke.

"They are not stupid, and please refrain from calling them that in front of Lady Regina. She thinks highly of her birds."

"Well, then, can I at least go talk to that stableboy named Fred? I don't have any friends my age and he seems nice."

"Not now." Hunter was still upset by what happened, or rather what didn't happen between him and Regina last night. He wanted her to trust him. He had wanted to kiss her again, and he could have sworn she wanted to kiss him as well. They'd made such a connection to each other, staring into each other's eyes. He supposed he'd assumed too much. Because instead of kissing, she only fired questions at him left and right. She also never seemed quite satisfied with his answers.

She doesn't want you and never will, came that evil voice in his head. *You aren't acting proper around her. She is a lady. You are just a commoner who drops his breeches at the bat of an eye. Nay, Hunter. She doesn't want you.*

Hunter was afraid his dear departed sister might be right this time. He would never be good enough for the regal, beautiful, intoxicating Lady Regina Blake. Why would she even ever be interested in someone like him? She wouldn't. Still, he couldn't stop thinking of her.

Even after his dip in the cold lake he still felt hot and bothered all night long. Hell, if he'd had even a few hours of sleep last night he'd be surprised. Why did this woman affect him in such a manner? Mayhap it was because she was a noble and he knew she was off limits to him. Hunter always had a longing for things he knew he couldn't have.

Not unlike Luke with all his wishes for things no commoner should ever own.

"Why couldn't I bring my sword with me? I don't want to leave it in our room. I want to show it off to the other boys my age." Luke continued to complain, making Hunter's brain throb. The hurting of his head never seemed to let up.

Both Hunter and the boy wore tunics and breeches and even shoes that were meant for a noble. Robin had made sure to leave the clothes for them so they would blend in. The tunic Luke wore was too big on him, looking ridiculous. The one Hunter wore was too small. It was tight and uncomfortable. The breeches were even worse. He was only thankful for the cloak covering him because the breeches were already straining on his body and he'd yet to even see Lady Regina today. If they got any tighter they would prob- ably split.

"Nay, we need to keep our weapons in our chamber from now on unless we leave the castle. They will only raise suspicion." Hunter still had his dagger on him and a dirk hidden in his boot. He didn't like going anywhere without protection, but didn't think his weapons were appropriate in the mews since they'd probably just scare the birds. Neither were they needed inside the castle walls being around all these knights. He was trying his best to blend in, but felt like anyone with a brain in their head would notice that he and Luke didn't belong here. It had to be more than obvious that even with his addlepated story of being Regi- na's cousin, that they weren't nobles at all.

"Hunter, over here," he heard the voice, looking up to see the falconer's assistant waving him over, standing just outside the mews. Hunter hurried over.

"Good morning, Roger," he said, noticing another man in the doorway of the mews with his back toward him. He looked to be sweeping. "Hello, there," he called out. The man worked cleaning up bird droppings with a broom and didn't even turn around.

"That is Cassian. He's almost deaf so you need to speak loudly," instructed Roger. "Cassian, Hunter said hello," the boy shouted. Finally, the old man turned around.

"Oh, good morning," said Cassian raising his wrinkled face to Hunter. He nodded quickly.

Hunter froze. He recognized this man. This was the master falconer back in the days when Hunter's father still worked here at the castle. Cassian had to be really old by now since he'd seemed old way back then. Since Hunter was just a lad the last time he'd been here, he hoped Cassian wouldn't recognize him.

"I'm Lord Hunter," he said, not using his surname since it was the same as his late father's. He also didn't want to keep saying his surname was Blake since it just didn't feel right. Growing up, his mother had insisted Hunter go by the name of Chase because that is who he was. Hunter always knew it was really because his stepfather despised him and didn't want another man's bastard using his surname.

"Yes, and I'm Cassian," said the man, turning back around and continuing to sweep. He didn't seem very friendly. Then again, if Hunter had once been a master falconer and was now sweeping up bird droppings he probably wouldn't be smiling either.

"Where is Lady Regina?" Hunter asked Roger, scanning the surrounding area but not seeing her.

"She went to the kitchen to get the food pouch for training," Roger explained. "Oh, here she comes now. Excuse me, but she'll want the bird so I need to get it."

"Yes. Yes, of course," said Hunter, turning to see Regina coming from the keep. She was smiling and talking to the woman who Hunter had seen sitting up on the dais yesterday. "Good morning, my lady." Hunter bowed, noticing Luke pouting and kicking at the ground. "Luke, it is proper to bow in the presence of ladies."

"I forgot." Luke bowed but said nothing to the women.

"Hunter, you're late," snapped Regina.

"I apologize, my lady. I didn't sleep very well and couldn't seem to get up this morning."

"Well, you're up now, right?"

When he saw the smirk on Regina's face as well as the other woman's, he realized just what he'd said and how she was probably thinking about what happened last night down at the lake. He didn't appreciate her snide comment, nor the fact she'd obviously told her friend all about it.

"I am Lady Sage, Robin's wife," the woman with Regina introduced herself. "I'm sorry I didn't get to meet you last night, but you weren't at the meal."

"I apologize, Lady Sage." Hunter stepped forward and took her hand, bringing it to his mouth in a kiss. "I am honored to be in the presence of the lady of the castle."

Sage giggled and looked over at Regina. Regina wasn't smiling.

"This is my nephew, Luke." Hunter released Sage's hand and nodded toward Luke.

"Nice to meet you, Luke," said Sage, sounding so friendly and as if she were going out of her way to be nice. "Isn't it a beautiful day?"

"I guess. Why does it matter?" Luke crossed his arms and continued to kick at the dirt. "I have to spend all day watching dumb birds."

"Luke, that's enough," warned Hunter. "Show some respect. What are you thinking?"

"I don't know what I'm thinking. I'm so hungry that I can't even think."

"Didn't you eat this morning?" Sage asked the boy.

"Nay. My uncle wouldn't let me." Luke glared at Hunter. "I can't even show anyone my sword. This isn't any fun at all."

"It's not supposed to be fun," Hunter told him. "We're here for a purpose and don't forget that. Lady Regina, we are ready to work."

Regina looked over at Sage and they exchanged glances. Regina had told her sister-by-marriage all about Hunter and how handsome he was. She also told him that Hunter was having trouble bringing up the boy on his own.

"There has been a change in plans," she announced.

"Really? What, Lady Regina?" asked Hunter.

"Since Luke is too young to be training as a falconer, I'm afraid he'll only be a distraction to the birds."

"So, what are you saying?" asked Hunter, looking confused.

"I suggest that during Luke's stay here he finds a different job to do."

"You do?" Luke looked up, suddenly interested. "Like what?"

"Oh, I don't know. What do you think, Sage?"

"Let me see." Sage tapped her chin with the tip of her finger. "Is there anything you like to do?"

"I like to practice fighting with my sword. Can I practice with the knights?" Luke's eyes opened wide in excitement.

"Luke, stop it," warned Hunter. "The knights don't want you getting in their way."

"No one seems to want me." Luke was back to being difficult.

"Lady Sage, isn't Robin going to be training his knights in the practice yard today?" asked Regina. "Mayhap Luke would like to watch."

"Would I!" Luke was so excited his brows soared and a smile spread clear across his face. "How do I get there?"

"I can take you," Sage offered. "But first we'll need to stop in the great hall and get a little something to eat. I'm finally feeling better but only if I eat a little something every few hours."

"We're going to eat? I'm hungry, too! Come on, let's go." Luke took Sage by the arm and started to pull her toward the keep.

"Remember, you're just watching the knights and that is all," Hunter called out after him. "Leave the sword in your room and stay out of their way. Do you hear me?"

"I hear you," grumbled Luke, hurrying toward the keep with Sage.

Hunter looked over at Regina. "Thank you."

"For what?" asked Regina, her eyes dancing with amusement.

"For helping me with the boy. Now, at least, mayhap he'll stop complaining so much and give my poor head a break."

"Hunter, I was serious about what I said. What we're about to do is not for children. It could be truly dangerous. Remember, these are birds of prey."

"I remember," said Hunter, thinking of the way the bird last night acted like it wanted to take off his head when he'd tried to pet it.

"I promise, you will see me do things that you've never seen anyone do before."

"Really?" Hunter liked the sound of that. "And what, my lady, might one of those things be?" Was she purposely playing with him and trying to get him aroused? He stared down at her, wanting to eat her up. He liked a woman with spirit not to mention a playful nature. This one had mischief written all over her face.

"You'll find out in time."

"Will I be able to join in on what you are going to do?" He grinned.

"Oh, I don't think you're skilled enough. But you are more than welcome to watch." She licked her lips, about driving him mad. Then she turned and headed to the mews leaving him standing there with sultry promises floating around in his head and his mouth hanging open.

"Oh, no, my lady," he said to himself. "Like hell if you think I'm just watching." He followed her to the mews trying to ignore the seductive sway of her hips that she probably had no idea she was even doing. Damn, this was going to be a long day.

～

"Be sure to stand back when you watch because what I'm going to do is dangerous," said Regina once they'd ridden to an open field used for training the birds that was close to the castle but not inside the castle walls.

"I understand," answered Hunter, not really understanding but wanting to be agreeable.

Regina had Hera, her gyrfalcon on her glove today. She'd told Hunter this was the largest and oldest of her birds. Hunter hadn't even been in the mews yet and wasn't even sure how many birds the mews housed or how many birds Regina owned.

"I'll help you from your horse, my lady." By the time he slid off his horse, she had already dismounted, managing to keep the bird balanced on her hand. She reached over and gave him the reins of her horse.

"Be sure to secure the horses a good distance away. I don't want them to frighten Hera."

"Of course, my lady." Hunter secured the reins of the horses to a tree and followed her to the center of the open field.

"Today, you'll see me use this." She used her free hand to pull something out of her pouch. At first glance it looked like feathers attached to a rope and wound up around a wooden handle. All he could think of was the whore he'd once spent the night with who enjoyed spanking and whipping, and odd things that did not interest him in the least.

"You weren't jesting when you said this was going to be dangerous."

"What did you say?" she asked, looking over her shoulder at him.

"Nothing," he remarked, not really sure what was about to happen. "What is that thing?"

"This is the lure," she told him.

"Yep," he said, swallowing deeply, thinking that is what the whore called her sex toys, too.

"Oh, so you've heard of it then?" she asked in surprise.

"Probably not in the same manner you mean. Why don't you explain it to me."

"Of course." She handed it to him. "Hold it while I remove Hera's hood. I took feathers to make it seem like a bird she'd be hunting in the sky. And to the feathers I attached a piece of raw meat. It is all attached to a rope that I will whirl around in the air."

When he took it, he realized it was a device used for training birds, and not a sex toy after all. It was a line wrapped around a heavy weighted handle.

"Why did you name the bird Hera?" he asked, watching her expertly remove the bird's hood with one hand while keeping Hera balanced on the other.

"I name all my birds after things to do with the sky. Hera was the wife of Zeus, the god of the sky, lightning and thunder. You know, in Greek mythology."

"Oh, yes," he said, not really knowing anything about mythology at all. He knew how to read and write, fight, and also how to grow crops. He wasn't skilled in book knowledge or literature of any kind. Instead, his skills had to do with fighting and tracking and hunting and killing.

"Thank you," she said, taking the lure from him. She sent the bird into the air. Hera lifted off her hand and took up into the sky. It was magical to watch the bird's wings span out as she soared through the air almost as if she were floating. This bird was a much bigger bird than the one he'd seen her with last night. The bird was also a lot more impressive. "I'll attach a piece of raw meat to the end of the lure now." She dug into her food bag and did so.

"Got anything cooked in there?" he mumbled, feeling his empty stomach growl, stretching his neck to see inside the bag.

"Pardon me?"

"Nothing. Go ahead," he said with a nod. "Continue."

"There is a certain way to do this but it takes a long time to learn. I don't see the point of even teaching you since you are not really going to be a falconer at all."

"You spin it around in the air, right?"

"Yes. This teaches the bird to hunt other birds and catch them in midflight."

"I'm watching," he said, taking a step back when she started to swing the lure around in the air over her head.

"Timing and accuracy is of utmost importance. I don't want the falcon to have to fly too close to me. I have to be sure to toss the lure out when she gets close."

"Why is that?"

"These birds can fly very fast, and even dive through the sky at great speeds," she said swinging the rope with the lure around her body and even spinning her body around from time to time. She seemed to do figure eights on one side of her body and then the other. "I don't want the bird or myself to get hurt. Now move further back. Here she comes."

Hunter did as instructed. He watched in awe as the bird flew back and forth making circles overhead. Regina continued to whirl the lure in the air around her, doing what she told him was a left-handed pass that was not as close to her body as a right-handed one. It was like a beautiful dance with the lure whirling through the air to one side and then the other. The bird flew back and forth swooping down and then going back up into the air again to try it all over.

After about a dozen passes, when Hera returned, Regina brought her arms together and threw the lure straight up in the sky, letting go of the rope altogether. Hera's talons grabbed onto the lure in midflight. Holding it, she drifted slowly to the ground never letting the lure go.

"Come on," said Regina, rushing over to the falcon.

"Why did you let go of the lure?" he asked, not understanding her method.

"I did that purposely so Hera wouldn't get hurt. The weight of the handle is too heavy for her to carry away and it gently guides her to the ground. Now, as her reward, I will give her a piece of raw meat. She'll let the lure loose so I can have it, and get back on my glove where she has been trained to go. I am careful never to feed the birds too much or they would have no desire to return to me."

Hunter was impressed. The bird did exactly as she said.

"You are quite a talented woman, Regina." He held nothing but admiration for her, watching her work as a falconer.

"Lady Regina," she corrected him.

"Pardon me?"

"I am a noblewoman. You must be sure to use my title, so don't forget again."

Any attraction between them was brought to an abrupt halt at that. Just like that lure being stopped in midair and brought right down to the ground.

CHAPTER 6

"Regina, you are so quiet today. Is something wrong?" asked Sage the next morning as they sat in the ladies solar stitching.

"Nay. Nothing's wrong." Regina flashed a smile at Sage and the other women, aimlessly pulling the colored thread through the bag she was embroidering.

"Really?" Sage reached out and picked up the bag. "Then why does this flower look more like a bird dropping?"

"Oh!" Regina had been thinking of Hunter and not even paying attention to what she was doing. "Well, you know I was never any good at this."

"And neither were you ever so bad either." Sage gave her that knowing look that said she knew Regina was keeping something from her.

"Will you be teaching your cousin falconry today?" asked Lady Jean who was a young widow.

"I—I suppose," she answered. "But I have so many other things to do."

"Your cousin, Hunter is sooooo handsome," gushed Lady Penelope who was about Regina's age and who always had eyes for the men. "Will you introduce me to him?"

"Me, too!" piped up yet another lady in the room, Lady Gertrude. She was old and had no business even looking Hunter's way.

"If I get the chance, of course, I will."

"Good," said Penelope with a giggle. "Because I am going to do my best to get him to kiss me."

"What?" Regina looked up quickly in surprise.

"I'd like to lure him to my bed and make hot, passionate love with him," said Jean looking like she was hot and bothered.

"What kind of a thing is that to say?" gasped Regina.

"Well, I'm a widow and don't need to protect my image anymore like you, Regina," said Jean. "I haven't had a man in a while and there is nothing wrong in wanting to find release."

"Oh, my," muttered Regina, fumbling with the needle, trying to get it back through the cloth with no result despite her best efforts.

"Ladies, a man like Lord Hunter won't want either of you," said Lady Gertrude. "He will need a more experienced woman in his bed. Like me and all the things I can show him." Lady Gertrude smacked her lips, almost turning Regina's stomach at the mere thought of this old woman in bed with Hunter.

"He's not looking for a woman, I'm sure, so please everyone just leave him be." Regina looked down at her work. She'd truly made a mess of the embroidery and would have to tear it all out and start over again. Why was it so hard to focus lately? And why were these lust-filled ladies targeting Hunter? Regina didn't want to share and felt like she wanted the man all to herself.

"Why wouldn't he be looking for a woman?" asked Jean, batting her eyes. "Or have you already claimed him for your-self, Regina?"

"Huh?" This startled her so much that she pricked her finger with the needle, enough to draw blood. "Ouch!" She threw the embroidery to the side and stood up. "Hunter is my cousin," she ground out. "I hardly think I'd be wanting to bed him but neither should you. Leave the man alone!"

"Just because he's your cousin, that doesn't mean a thing," said Jean. "A lot of nobles marry their cousins. It keeps the bloodline strong. He is so handsome, I don't see why you don't want him, too."

"Did you say marry?" Regina wasn't sure she liked where this conversation was leading.

"Jean, don't give her ideas," scolded Penelope. "I hear the man already has eyes for Regina. If they couple, we'll never have a chance with him at all."

"Hunter has eyes for me? Where did you hear that?" This shocked Regina that the gossip had gotten to this point so fast. She only hoped that no one had seen them down at the lake.

Penelope continued. "The scullery maid told me she was washing dishes in the lake last night and saw you and Hunter by the water together. She said she saw Hunter stark naked!"

"Really? Naked?" Jean's eyes lit up with excitement and she squirmed in her chair.

"What do you mean?" exclaimed Regina, her breath hitching in her throat.

"Is this true, Regina?" asked Sage, sounding as shocked to hear them say this as she was.

"I—I..." Regina didn't know how to answer. This was how gossip started. Even if it wasn't really gossip but the truth. Still, if it wasn't stopped immediately, Regina's reputation as a lady would be ruined. If that happened, no nobleman would ever want her someday as his wife.

"The scullery maid said Hunter has quite a nice...body. In every way." Jean's smile widened and both she and Penelope squealed.

"I'd like to see that," said Gertrude, a sly smile turning up the corners of her mouth.

"Ladies!" Sage stood up with hand on her belly. "That will be all. Now, I do not want to hear another word about this silly nonsense. It is idle gossip and will go no further than this room. We are ladies and must conduct ourselves as such. Do you all understand?" It was ironic that Sage was the one telling the others to act like ladies when Sage wasn't noble born but had only inherited the title of lady when she'd married Robin.

The ladies nodded to Sage and their smiles disappeared. They turned their attention back to their stitching once again.

Flushed and flustered, Regina threw down her embroidery and ran from the room.

"Regina, wait!" Sage called after her, following her out of the ladies solar.

"I need to get to the mews, Sage." Regina spoke without

turning around for fear her sister-by-marriage would see the blush rising to her cheeks. She walked faster.

"Regina, please. I still don't feel that well and cannot run to keep up with you."

"Oh, I'm sorry. I forgot about that." Regina turned and headed back down the corridor and put her hand on Sage's shoulder. "Is there anything I can get for you?"

"Nay. I'm fine." Sage's breathing was a little labored but she still managed a smile for Regina, always seeming to care for others more than herself. "Walk and talk with me," said Sage, holding on to Regina's arm and strolling down the corridor at a much slower pace. "These walls have ears, you realize. Always be careful what you do or say." Sage looked back over her shoulder as she said it. Regina looked back to see both Ladies Penelope and Jean peeking out the solar door, watching them, probably hoping to hear something to use for tomorrow's gossip.

"Yes, you're right," she agreed, turning as they continued down the hall.

"It seems Hunter Chase has been making quite a stir around Shrewsbury Castle since his arrival," commented Sage.

"Yes. I suppose so."

"How much of that gossip is true?"

Regina stopped and turned toward Sage. She let out a deep sigh, not wanting to lie to her. "Most of it," she answered softly.

"What? Really?" Sage's eyes opened wide. "I don't understand."

"I was flying Lightning down at the lake the other night.

Hunter was there and approached me. He was half-naked, meaning to go for a swim."

"Half-naked?" Sage couldn't hold back her amusement. "Well, that just shows how gossip elaborates on things. Those ladies said he was totally naked."

"Well…he was."

Sage's mouth dropped open and she was barely able to speak. "What?"

"When I was about to leave, he stripped down and took a swim in the lake. But it wasn't until I was already walking away, I swear."

"Oh, Regina, you had better hope Robin doesn't hear about this. It can only bring you trouble."

"Nothing happened between us, Sage. Honest."

Sage let out another breath. "Well, that's good that he didn't try to kiss you or touch you."

"Right. Not there at the lake, anyway," she mumbled under her breath, turning and continuing to walk.

"Wait a minute, Regina." Sage hurried to catch up to her, grabbing her arm and spinning her around. "You cannot dump that on me and then just think you are going to walk away. You'd better explain and do it fast because I am losing my patience."

"There is nothing to explain." Regina shrugged. "Hunter kissed me, but it was before he ever came to the castle. Besides, Robin already knows about it, so you can stop worrying."

"What is going on between you two?" Sage blinked several times in succession.

"Nothing at all."

"That isn't what it sounds like. What did you do when Hunter kissed you?"

"I slapped him, of course. And reprimanded him for even thinking he had the right to kiss a noble."

"Regina, remember that I wasn't a noble before I married Robin. I never liked the haughtiness of those born into a higher status and I still don't. If you keep acting like that, you are going to push the man away."

"Good. Because he is here to do a job and that job has nothing to do with kissing anyone. Especially not a noblewoman."

"Ah, there you are," came Hunter's voice, causing Regina to spin around. Hunter and Robin walked toward her from the great hall. "I was starting to think you were avoiding me for some reason."

She *was* trying to avoid him because spending so much time with him was making her mind confused. This man was nothing but trouble. He was here under false pretense to do a job and he wasn't doing it.

"There will be no training session at the mews today," she told him, keeping her composure even though he looked handsome as always. However, he was wearing his own clothes and no longer dressed like a noble. "Why did you change your clothes? Those are not the ones you were wearing yesterday."

"Robin's clothes were too tight on me," he told her. "They were catching too much interest from all the ladies at the castle so I put mine back on. Why? Did you like seeing me in those tighter breeches?" He held a dung-eating smile on his face and the conversation only made her blush even more.

"They are not the clothes of a noble," she told him. "However, as long as you cover your body, I don't really care what you wear." She wanted to tell him about the scullery maid having seen him naked and all the gossip, but she couldn't do it with her brother standing right there. It would turn out badly for both of them if Robin discovered she'd been alone with a naked man. Even if they didn't do anything.

"I will summon my Uncle William to the castle to make something appropriate for you," Robin told Hunter.

"Thank you," said Hunter, his attention going back to Regina.

"Why not?" he asked her, folding his arms over his chest.

"What do you mean?" She started to become nervous, thinking he was going to say something about her wanting to see him naked or some such nonsense.

"Why will there be no training at the mews today?"

"Oh, that." Relief swept through her. "I figured that you'll never catch the thief if you don't spend time looking for the culprit. And I can assure you, that you won't find the thief in the mews."

"She has a point," agreed Robin. "Actually, Regina, that is exactly what Hunter and I were just talking about."

"You were?"

"Yes. I've decided the ploy of him being a falconer's assistant isn't believable. My men are starting to ask questions. Mayhap I'll have him spend more time in the great hall and amongst the nobles instead. I think that might be more beneficial."

"I suppose so since he won't be able to actually train or even touch the birds," agreed Regina, even though she didn't like the idea of Hunter not being with her. She was starting to like having him around.

"Good morning, Hunter," came a sultry voice, interrupting them.

"Ladies," said Hunter with a nod as Penelope, Jean, and Gertrude walked up and stopped before them. "How are you this fine day?"

"I am Lady Jean and would be better with a kiss on the hand." Jean boldly reached out for him. Hunter took her hand and kissed it.

"Me too," said Penelope, pushing her hand in front of Hunter's face. "I am Lady Penelope." He kissed her hand as well.

"What about you, my lady?" Hunter looked up and gave Gertrude a smile that would make any woman blush.

"Ladies, continue on to the great hall," instructed Sage, coming to her rescue. "We are in the middle of an important conversation."

"Of course," said Jean, giggling and whispering behind her hand as she and the other ladies walked away. For some reason, Hunter kissing their hands bothered Regina. Still, she couldn't show it.

"Hunter, Hunter, look at what I have!" Luke ran up with the stableboy Fred on his heels. In Luke's arms was a black cat that had a small white spot on one of her front paws. "We found her in the stable today. Fred said she is probably a stray and that she doesn't belong to anyone. Can I keep her? Can I?"

· · ·

Hunter groaned inwardly when she saw his nephew with the cat. "I said no pets, Luke. Now put the cat back where you found her."

"I'm going to name her Inky." Luke didn't listen to a word he said. "Fred, do you think more stray cats might wander into the stable? Mayhap Inky needs a friend."

"We can watch for them," said Fred. "There are always so many mice, that the cats would really help us out."

"Luke, you're not listening to me," said Hunter softly, trying not to cause havoc.

"Mayhap we should go to the kitchen and get something for Inky to eat," suggested Luke.

"Good idea," agreed Fred. "I think most cats like meat. Follow me." The boys ran off, leaving Hunter standing there feeling like a fool. God's teeth, why wouldn't the boy listen to him?

"I think I'll start my investigation in the stables today," Hunter told the others. "Tell me again. Which one of the knights had his horse stolen?"

"It was Sir Elwood," Sage supplied the information.

"And where would I find Sir Elwood?" asked Hunter.

"I can introduce you to him," Robin offered. "As well as the guard who had his sword stolen. Mayhap they can give you some insight of what actually happened."

"Yes, that will be a good start. My ladies," said Hunter with a bow. "I will let you continue with your conversation."

"You don't need to bow to us," said Sage. She leaned forward and spoke in a hushed voice. "After all, you are a noble too now, remember."

"Oh. Yes, I suppose you are right." Hunter wasn't sure about this. He would feel as if he were disrespecting the nobles if he didn't, but supposed he needed to keep up appearances. He wasn't sure he'd ever get used to this act of pretending to be a noble.

"So, Robin. Hunter is no longer going to be spending time in the mews?" asked Regina, surprising Hunter that she was even asking as if she cared. He thought she'd be jumping for joy not to have to be around him.

"Nay, I thought we just covered that," said Robin. "You said you agreed."

"That's right," broke in Hunter. "There seems to be no need for me in the mews since you so clearly pointed out that I would not find this thief by spending time there."

"True, but my birds might be in danger," she blurted out. "I think it would be a good thing if Hunter didn't stray far. I mean, in case he is needed."

"Ah, yes." Hunter stroked his beard. "But the question is, will I be in danger too? I mean, I don't take a fancy to being slapped around."

Hunter was toying with her, but saw that she wasn't in a playful mood this morning. Her brows dipped and she frowned at him.

"Never mind. I don't need his help. I will be in the mews if anyone is looking for me." She turned and bolted off, leaving Hunter dumbfounded.

"I said the wrong thing, didn't I?" Hunter asked Robin. "I was only jesting, trying to lighten the mood."

"I'm not sure," said Robin. The men watched Regina storm through the corridor nearly knocking into several servants along the way. "I gave up knowing just why women do or say anything. It never makes a bit of sense to me."

"Robin, stop being so insensitive," scolded Sage. "Can't you two tell that Regina's feelings were hurt?"

"Hurt? I hurt her? How?" For the life of him, Hunter didn't know how to act around the girl. One minute Regina was kissing him with passion and seeming like she enjoyed it. The next, she was slapping him or storming away in a huff. "What do you think is bothering her?" Hunter scratched the back of his neck in thought.

"With Regina, one never knows." Robin shrugged. "I wouldn't worry about it. She's probably having her flux and should stop being so grouchy in a few days."

"You both are truly simpkins, aren't you?" snapped Sage.

Hunter and Robin looked at each other in confusion but didn't dare say a word. Sage was pregnant with twins and it probably wouldn't be wise to upset her.

"The poor girl has already spent the morning as the brunt of gossip because you can't keep your breeches on, Hunter. Haven't you caused her enough trouble already?" Sage stormed away as well.

"Thief-taker, is there something you want to tell me?" Robin shot him a daggered look.

"Nay. Not really," he said, turning to walk away. Hunter stopped and looked back at Robin and held up a finger. "Except, who do I speak to about getting a bath sent to my chamber in the future?"

CHAPTER 7

After talking to Sir Elwood and not being able to get any information that would help Hunter find the thief, he decided to take a walk to the stables. Mayhap the old groom would have seen or heard something that would help shed light on the stolen horse at least.

"Hello?" he called out, walking into the stables, letting his eyes get accustomed to the dim light. "Are you here, Al?" He didn't hear an answer, so decided to look around while he waited for the man to return.

Hunter walked from stall to stall, petting each of the horses on the nose. Then he came to the stall that held Luke's horse. "Hello, Zelma, how are you today?" He opened the gate and walked in to pet the horse.

"Who are you calling Zelma?" grumbled Al, stepping out from behind the horse with a brush in his hand.

"Al," said Hunter in surprise. "I didn't think you were here."

"Of course, I am. This is where I work. Where did you expect me to be?"

"I called out for you when I entered the stable but you didn't answer."

"It's hard to hear anything way back here. What did you want?"

"I wanted to talk to you about Sir Elwood's stolen horse."

"What about it?" he grumbled.

Hunter reached up and pet the horse on the nose. "I was just wondering if you heard anything odd or saw anyone suspicious the day Sir Elwood's horse was stolen."

"Why do you want to know? How is it any of your business?"

The man was cocky and crusty. It made Hunter think he had something to hide.

"I don't believe you'd want Lord Robin to know the way you are talking to a noble, would you?"

"Sorry, my lord." The man continued to brush the horse. "It's just that I keep forgettin' you're noble. You look so much like someone else."

"Like who?" he asked nonchalantly, pushing aside some strands of hair from the horse's eyes.

"I don't know. I can't remember. But whoever it was, I know he wasn't a noble."

"It seems to me that you're mistaken, Al. Now, what can you tell me about the stolen horse?"

"Nothing about Sir Elwood's horse, but I can tell you that this horse was stolen." He nodded at Zelma.

"Really? Why would you say that?" Hunter slowly ran a hand over the horse's flank.

"Because of these trappings," he said, reaching out and touching the horse's bridle. "See these decorations etched into the leather? Well, I've only seen this once before. It was on the horse of a lord who visited here years ago. The lord was from Sheffield. His name was Lord Bohun."

"Really. Years ago?" asked Hunter. "Like how long?"

"Mayhap ten years or so."

"That is a long time to remember something. Perhaps you are mistaken."

"Nay, I'm not."

"All I can tell you is that this is my nephew's horse. It was given as part of a payment from a man who owed me money."

"What kind of debt could require such an expensive thing like a horse?"

"That, my friend, is my business and you need not concern yourself with it."

"Where did the man get the horse from? Did he steal her?" The man cocked his head and looked at Hunter from the side of his eyes.

"I assure you that I know darned well the man whom I received this horse from did not steal her. If I remember correctly, he might have gotten her from Lord Bohun, actually. Now, excuse me, but I have things I need to do. Please take good care of my nephew's horse for him."

"Aye, my lord," said the man to Hunter's back. Hunter couldn't wait to leave the stables because if he stayed here any longer, the man was going to start a rumor that Hunter was the thief.

~

"Cassian, to where did Roger disappear? I am guessing he took Cloud out to fly since the bird is gone too," said Regina, tending to her birds in the mews. Cassian's back was to her as he scrubbed the crusty empty perch. He didn't answer.

Regina finished putting the hood on Hera and walked over to the man, resting her hand on his shoulder. He jumped and turned around.

"I'm sorry to have frightened you," she told the old, nearly-deaf man. "Did Roger take Cloud out to the flying field? I didn't ask him to do that."

"Oh, I'm not sure," said Cassian. "I was in my room." The old man slept in the attached room to the mews. Roger stayed here sometimes and other times went to be with his family in the village.

"Did you hear him come in?" she asked. "Actually, I thought he was going to get here late today since he stayed with his family in the village last night."

"I didn't hear nothin,'" said the man.

"Of course not," she answered with a sigh, realizing the man couldn't hear anyone unless they were basically yelling. "Did you tend to the birds this morning since Roger wasn't here?"

"Of course, my lady."

"Was Cloud here at the time?"

"Nay, he wasn't. I thought you took him."

"What do you mean? I was in the ladies solar all morning. Where is my falcon?" she demanded to know. Her heart started to race. If anything happened to any of her birds, she would just die. Panic started to consume her.

"Good morning, Lady Regina," she heard from behind

her. She spun around to find Roger walking into the mews with Cloud perched atop his falconer's glove.

"Oh, thank goodness!" she cried, hurrying over to him. "I was so afraid something had happened to Cloud."

"I returned early from the village and decided to let him fly this morning since it was such a beautiful sky. I hope you don't mind."

"I don't mind as long as you tell someone you're taking the bird."

"I did," said Roger. "I told Cassian."

"Really." She turned to look back at Cassian. The man's back was toward them and he was banging the brush against a bucket, startling the perched, hooded birds. "Cassian, stop making that noise. You are frightening the birds."

"I'm afraid he doesn't hear the noise so doesn't know that." Roger put Cloud back on his perch. "His hearing seems to be getting worse lately."

"Aye," she answered, speaking aloud since the man couldn't hear them anyway. "I'm not sure a man with little to no hearing belongs working in the mews. I need someone more like you who will be sure to protect the birds."

"Protect? What do you mean?" asked Roger.

"Don't say anything to anyone, Roger, but there have been burglaries right here at the castle lately."

"Really? I can't believe that," said Roger. "Why doesn't Lord Robin do something about it?"

"He is."

"What?"

She could have kicked herself for telling the boy anything at all. Regina realized she was being no different than Lady Penelope or Lady Jean, spreading gossip. "Never mind," she said. "Just please stay close to the birds from now on."

"Of course, my lady. Do you think this thief might try to steal one of the hunting birds?"

"Anything is possible, but let's hope not."

"Lady Regina, Lady Sage sent us to find you." Luke walked into the mews with Fred. He carried the stray cat.

"Luke, you can't bring that cat in here," gasped Regina. Already, her birds sensed the feline and even though they were hooded, they started to become restless.

"Inky won't hurt them," said Luke, petting the cat. "She's a good girl."

"Nay, you don't understand. These are hunting birds, Luke. They hunt prey bigger than that cat. This isn't a safe environment for Inky."

"She's right," said Roger. "You'd better take the cat back to the barn."

"Nay," protested Luke. "I am bringing Inky with us."

"With you? Where are you going?" asked Regina.

"On an outing."

"What kind of outing?" she asked.

"The one that we're going on with you. That is why Sage sent me to fetch you." He reached out and took Regina's hand, pulling her toward the door.

"I'd better get back to work in the stables," said Fred. "My grandfather won't be happy that I've been gone so long."

"Yes, you'd better," said Regina as Luke pulled her out the door and to a horse and wagon that was waiting. On the bench seat sat Sage and Robin. Their one-and-a-half year old little boy, Martin, was sitting between them.

"Hello, Regina. Hurry up and get in the wagon," instructed Sage.

"What? Why?" she asked, thinking this was so odd.

"We are going on a little outing and taking you with us since it is such a nice day," Robin told her.

Regina considered getting away, but then thought she'd be in the way since Sage and Robin might want to be alone with their child. Just their little family. "Thank you, but I think I'll stay here."

"Inky and I are going." Luke jumped in the back of the wagon and put the cat down in the hay that was covering the bottom of the cart. The cat batted and swatted at a fly and jumped up in the air, landing covered in hay.

"Please, Regina," begged Sage. "You seem upset today and I think some time out in the fresh air and open areas away from the castle will be good for you."

"Unless you're forgetting, I spend time in open areas and in the fresh air every day with my birds," she told her sister-by-marriage.

"Today you'll do it without your birds," Sage told her. "Now get in." She said it in such a commanding tone that Regina obeyed, climbing in the back of the wagon with the boy. The cat hurried over and settled atop her lap.

"Oh, my, you're a friendly one," she said, running her hand over the kitten's back as Robin drove the cart and they started to move.

"Yes, I've been called friendly on more than one occasion by a pretty woman," came Hunter's voice as he ran up behind the wagon and jumped up. He pushed in right between her and Luke and sat down. "However, I can't say I've ever heard those words about me coming from your mouth before." That silly grin was on his face again. The three of them sat on the back of the wagon with their feet dangling over the open end.

"Hunter, what are you doing here?" asked Regina, still petting Inky.

"Same as you," he answered, taking the cat from her and putting Inky on his lap. When he did so, his hands brushed against hers, sending a spiral of excitement shooting through her.

"We're going on an outing to eat food down by the creek," Luke blurted out.

"Me, too," Hunter answered, running his fingers through the cat's fur, making the thing actually purr. The feline rubbed up against him.

"You weren't invited," said Regina, her heart racing just being so close to him.

"Hunter, aren't you supposed to be hunting down thieves today?" Robin called out from the front of the cart.

"I invited him, dear," Sage told her husband. "Everyone needs to stop and eat."

"Of course," mumbled Regina, knowing Sage was trying to get her to gush over Hunter the way the other ladies did this morning in the solar.

Regina looked over at the pregnant woman and mouthed the words *what are you doing?*

Sage mouthed the word back, *relax.*

"Luke, I told you no pets," said Hunter. "Mayhap we can lose this cat out in the woods."

"Nay!" screamed Luke, yanking Inky from him and moving up to the front of the wagon where he sat in the hay cradling her on his lap. Little Martin stood on the bench seat looking back at the kitten. Sage held the little boy steady.

"Don't you think that was rather mean?" asked Regina in a soft tone so Luke wouldn't hear her.

"Mean?" Hunter made a face that said he couldn't believe she was siding with the boy. "I am trying to get my nephew to obey me. I told him, no pets, yet he defied me."

"And you thought saying that would fix things, did you?" She crossed her arms over her chest and raised a brow.

"I didn't really mean I was going to dump the cat in the woods. I was just trying to...I mean I wanted to..."

"To rule by fear? That doesn't work with children, Hunter. Try love next time instead."

"I might not be a parent but neither are you. What would you know about children?"

"I might not be married, but I assure you, I know plenty about love," she ground out.

"Really." He looked into her eyes, making her feel like a prisoner since she was helpless to look away. His handsome face was close to her. His leg pressed up against hers, and his presence in her personal space felt invasive but at the same time enchanting. "I was talking about ruling by fear. However, since you assured me you know plenty about love, I'd like to hear more of your experiences."

"M–my experiences?" She looked up into his eyes, feeling as if he could see into her very soul. If he could, he would know that she'd never had any experiences with love. Not with a man. She'd always been too busy with her birds.

"Yes, your experiences. With love," he said in not more than a hot whisper. His gaze traveled down to her lips and her eyes went to his mouth as well. She couldn't stop thinking how those strong but sexy lips had felt against hers. How warm and sensuous they really were. Hunter had tasted of whisky and danger. It excited her. She'd almost melted to a puddle when he'd held her in his arms.

The wagon hit a bump in the road causing Regina's body to lift up into the air for a second. When she landed, she found herself wrapped in Hunter's protective embrace. To her surprise, her arms were around him too and her face was resting on his broad chest.

"You'd better hold on tightly, my lady." His deep voice rumbled in his chest and she felt the vibrations against her cheek. "These roads can get rough. We wouldn't want to lose you."

"Nay, we wouldn't want that," she repeated.

"And I don't want to lose Inky," Luke said from behind them, making Regina realize that the boy had probably heard every word spoken between them. She quickly pushed out of Hunter's embrace, scooting away from him until her back touched the side of the wagon. She didn't fear falling off, she just didn't want to be so close to this powerful, intoxicating man. The man who could seem to make her lose all common sense when she was anywhere near him. Especially wrapped in his strong arms.

"Hunter, how did things turn out with your inquiries regarding the stolen horse and sword?" Robin asked later as the group finished up eating, sitting on the blanket on the ground near the creek.

The food had been plentiful and delicious—still warm

meat pies, some fine roasted beef, mounds of cold, sliced chicken, a large round of cheese, fresh-baked bread, oatcakes and a small jar of newly-churned butter, then custard tarts, sugared almonds, a very good wine, and plenty of thirst-quenching ale. However, the best part of the outing had to be the view. Regina sat across from him being such a proper lady that he couldn't believe she was the same girl who had returned his kiss with so much passion the first time he'd met her.

"I'm sorry to say I came up empty-handed," Hunter answered. "No one could seem to tell me anything of value. No one admits to seeing anyone suspicious either."

"That's too bad." Robin took a swig of wine straight from the bottle and held it out to Hunter. Hunter shook his head and held up his hand, being satisfied with what he already had. "I had hoped you would have found some clues as to who is pilfering items within the castle by now. I am getting a little nervous that the thief might strike again soon."

"Don't worry. I will find the thief," promised Hunter. "Sometimes, these things just take a little time and can't be rushed."

"Perhaps Lady Sage can give you some insight on her stolen brooch." Regina made the suggestion. She daintily picked up a small piece of roasted beef in her fingers and brought it to her mouth. They'd all just used their hands to eat since the cook forgot to pack spoons and not a one of them remembered to bring along their eating knives. Most of the food was easily eaten using their fingers anyway.

Hunter chuckled.

"What is so funny?" Regina did that dainty thing again,

feeding herself much the same way that she fed her birds the raw meat. It was a reward for the birds, and a reward for Hunter just to watch her now.

"Nothing," he said, leaning back onto his elbows and stretching out in the sun. He didn't think she'd find his comparison amusing so thought it best not to state his thoughts aloud. "So, Lady Sage, where was the last place you saw this missing brooch?"

"It was on my dressing table. In the morning a few days ago, I believe." Sage had little Martin on her lap, giving him bread to eat. "I was going to wear it that day, but I wasn't feeling well. My handmaid didn't help me dress until mayhap noon. By then, I realized the brooch was missing."

"Do you trust the handmaid?" asked Hunter, taking another swig of ale from the pewter cup that had been packed with the food.

"Yes. Completely."

"What is her name?" asked Hunter.

"Her name is Clotilda."

"Is she married? Does she have children?" He asked the questions he normally asked on a thief finding mission.

"Nay. She's an older woman with no family remaining," said Sage. "She has no eye for baubles. As a matter of fact, Clotilda always tells me that jewelry is naught but a distraction from a lady's true beauty and charm."

Hunter looked over to Regina again who wore no jewelry at all. Then again, she didn't need it. Baubles would only take away from her natural glow. "I have to agree with the handmaid," he said, staring at Regina the entire time he spoke. Her eyes lifted and when she saw him looking at her she quickly lowered her gaze.

"It was a brooch that looked like a hawk flying in air," Sage continued. Martin fussed, reaching for the cat that Luke played with next to him. She put the boy down and he crawled over and tried to grab the cat's tail. "There were diamonds in the tips of the bird's wings and its eye was a ruby. It meant a lot to me."

"It sounds like a precious and expensive piece," commented Hunter.

"It was," Regina spoke up. "I helped Robin choose the brooch that he gave Sage for their wedding anniversary just last year."

"Of course, you did," he said, thinking Regina would be the only person he knew to suggest someone wear a brooch that looked like a bird of prey.

"Do you think you'll be able to find it for Sage?" asked Regina. "I'd hate to think something that means so much to her might be lost and gone forever."

"I'll do my best," said Hunter. "After all, that is what I'm here for." Some fool notion caused him to wink at Regina. That only seemed to startle her and he regretted the action as soon as he did it. Her cheeks flushed. She once again looked down to her lap rather than at him. Slowly, she wiped her fingers on a cloth.

"I had a scare today," mumbled Regina, surprising all of them with her words.

"What?" Hunter sat upright. "Was someone giving you a hard time? Tell me who it was." Since he knew about the ladies gossiping about his naked ass, he now felt bad that he hadn't returned to his chamber for a bath that night like Regina had suggested. After all, the last thing he wanted was to ruin her fine and unblemished reputation.

"Nay, no one tried to harm me if that's what you want to know. What I meant was that I thought one of my birds had been stolen."

"What are you saying?" This got Robin's attention quickly. "Has the thief struck again? Please tell me this isn't so."

"Nay, Robin, please calm down," said Regina, keeping her emotions steady. "Everything is fine. What happened was that Roger came and got Cloud from the mews and told Cassian he was taking the bird to fly him. Of course the old man is so deaf that he didn't hear him. That is what caused the misunderstanding."

"I swear, I should have let that man go like I wanted to when I first took over as lord of the castle," said Robin, getting up and brushing crumbs from his tunic. He reached down and picked up Martin just as the boy was about to pull the cat's tail. "Cassian's not any value to me at all. He can barely do the menial tasks you ask him to do, and he cannot hear worth a damn."

"He was the master falconer before Regina, right?" asked Hunter, gathering more information.

"Yes, he was," answered Regina. "I felt bad that Robin made me master falconer and took the position away from him. That is why I convinced Robin to let Cassian stay on and live in the small room just off of the mews that is used for storage. This way he could still help out whenever I needed him."

"Does he resent it?" asked Hunter, finishing off his ale and putting the cup down on the blanket.

"I don't know," said Regina. "He's never mentioned it if he does."

"I'm sure he's not happy about it," said Robin. "But as Lord Shrewsbury now I don't care. I can do whatever I please."

"What can you tell me about the stable groom, Alfred?" asked Hunter.

"Alfred the old or the young?" Robin asked, taking Martin and putting the boy on his shoulders. Martin laughed and pulled at Robin's hair.

"Old," said Hunter.

"I don't know much about him," Robin admitted. "He was the castle's groom when I took over and he seemed to do a good job. So I didn't change things where that was concerned."

"I see." Hunter stood up as well. The women cleaned up the food, putting the remnants back into the basket along with the blanket they'd sat on.

"I'm going to take Inky down by the creek for a drink of water," announced Luke.

"I'll go with you. I could use a walk," Hunter spoke up.

"Nay," spat Luke. "You will probably drown her." He hugged the cat closer in a protective manner, causing the animal to feel trapped and making her try to get away. The boy seemed to be resenting Hunter lately and that did not sit right with Hunter at all.

"God's eyes, Luke, what has gotten into you?" growled Hunter. "You are more obstinate now than ever before. You never acted this defiant, not even on any of our missions."

"I don't want to go on missions with you anymore," said the boy, surprising the hell out of Hunter. He had thought Luke loved the life of excitement and danger. The boy had always begged to go along with Hunter wherever he went.

"Fred is my friend now and I want to do things with him, not you."

"It sounds like Fred might be becoming a bad influence on you." Hunter didn't know where this sour attitude was coming from with his nephew. It only added to Hunter's growing problems and frustrations.

"Robin and I were planning to go for a walk down by the creek with Martin," Sage spoke up. "Martin likes throwing rocks into the water. Would it be all right if we came with you, Luke? To help look after Inky?" Hunter noticed that Sage spoke in a gentle and kind voice to Luke. She also asked the boy's permission to join him which is something Hunter would never do where a child was concerned.

"Yes, I'd like that," said Luke with a smile, easing up on holding the cat so tightly. "I'll race you down to the water."

"Sage, don't even think of running," warned Robin, grabbing her by the arm and holding Martin on his shoulders with his other hand. "You are pregnant and still not totally well. We don't want to risk you falling and getting hurt or possibly harming the babies."

"Stop fussing, Robin," Sage said with a smile on her face as if Robin's overprotectiveness amused her. "I wouldn't run and you know it."

They walked down to the water talking about Sage's condition as well as the safety of their unborn children.

"Well, I guess that just leaves us," Hunter told Regina with a clap of his hands. "What did you want to do?"

Her gaze shot over to him. For a moment she seemed to almost look frightened. "Nothing, with you," she said. "I think I will just sit here and soak up some sun." She took the basket from the food and started walking back to the wagon. Hunter could have kicked himself. He didn't like getting such a cold treatment from the wench and wasn't sure why she was acting this way. Or what he may have said wrong.

"Here, let me take that." He snatched the basket from her hand before she could object. "Regina, did I do or say something wrong?"

"I don't understand what you mean." They continued to walk.

"I get the feeling you are not happy with me."

"Why would you say that?"

They stopped at the wagon and Hunter slid the basket into the hay in the back. "It's because there is gossip going around the castle that you and I were together at night and I was naked, right?"

Her eyes opened wide in surprise. "What do you mean?"

"Don't play games with me, sweetheart. I know all about the ladies in the solar insinuating that you might have done something unladylike."

"Sage told you, didn't she?" Regina let out a deep sigh.

"Regina, can we sit and talk for a moment? There is something I'd like to say to you while we are alone."

Her eyes flashed down to the ground again and she wrung her hands together. That told Hunter that she was feeling uncomfortable around him.

"Please," he said in a soft voice. "I would like to clear the air between us."

"I suppose, it would be fine," she finally answered. "We can sit in the back of the wagon."

"Let me help you," he said, putting his hands around her waist and lifting her up.

. . .

Regina felt her heart soaring again just from Hunter's touch. She felt like one of her birds freely flying through the sky, drinking in the sun, the breeze, and everything that makes one feel good about life.

He put her down and released her and climbed into the wagon sitting beside her. Regina leaned back on her hands and dangled her feet in the air off the end of the wagon. "I like sitting on the back of wagons." One of her shoes came off and flew through the air, landing in the grass. That made them both laugh.

"I'll retrieve it," he told her but she stopped him.

"Nay, I like the feel of the air against my toes." She purposely kicked off the other shoe and it landed next to the first.

"You surprise me," he told her. "I didn't think ladies would purposely kick off their shoes. Especially in mixed company."

"It's not like I'm taking off clothes, like some people I know. It feels good. You should try it."

"Nay, I don't think so." He held up one hand and moved back a little.

"Why not?"

"Because the last time I removed clothing in your presence, it only seemed to cause problems, that's why."

She giggled. "I suppose you have a point. Now, what did you want to talk to me about?"

He was silent for a moment and then his smile disappeared. It seemed as if he became suddenly serious. "Never mind." He looked the other way. "It was nothing."

"No, tell me." She reached out and laid her hand on his arm. "It sounded so important a moment ago."

"It's probably not." He was closing himself off from her and it made her sad.

"Mayhap I should start," she told him.

"Huh?" He turned to look at her.

"I admit, it bothered me a little when the ladies started the gossip about us being together down by the lake."

"I'm sorry. That is all my fault. I sometimes do things before considering the consequences."

"Nay, don't apologize. Those ladies are haughty and would only have found something else to gossip about if it wasn't you."

"I don't suppose I'm making a very good impression, am I?"

"On the contrary, every one of them is infatuated with you. Especially since they've heard about you being naked."

"Really?" He looked at her from the corners of his eyes. "All of them?"

"Mmm hmm," she said with a nod. "Especially Lady Gertrude."

"Lady Gertrude?"

"The old one."

"Oooh. Oh!" He cringed and made a face, causing them both to laugh once again. "Regina, since we are talking about attraction, I must admit that I am very besotted with you."

Now it was her turn to say, "Oh!"

"Too bold of me to admit my feelings to you directly?"

"I suppose it is better than having to hear it from wagging tongues."

He slowly reached out and took her hand in his and she let him do it. "I know nothing can happen between us, but since I've met you I cannot stop thinking about you, my lady."

"Please, just call me Regina when we are alone." She interlocked her fingers with his, and they sat there holding hands.

"I'm not sure I can do that."

"Why not?" she asked. "I call you Lord Hunter in front of everyone, yet you are not even a noble."

"I know. That bothers me."

"Why? It is part of the ploy. Your alias. So you can do your job undetected."

"I suppose," he said, letting out a deep breath. "But there has been too much lying in my life. I'm afraid it might be leading Luke down the wrong path."

"Too much lying?"

He nodded. "I often rely on it when I do my work."

"So, it is needed."

"Not to get the job done. Just to get what I want."

"I don't understand." Hunter was confusing her again. Now, she started wondering if his words of attraction were only to get what he wanted with her as well.

"Never mind," he told her. "I just wanted to say that I am really enjoying spending time with you. So much so that I almost hope it takes me a long time to catch the thief."

"What? Why?"

"Because, that will give me more time to spend with you." He picked up her hand and kissed it, just like he kissed the hands of the other ladies in the castle.

"You kiss all the ladies, don't you?" She was starting to wonder about his charming ways.

"Only on the hand. Then again, you are different." He reached up and tucked a stray strand of hair behind her ear. It was an innocent act but affected her more than she wanted him to know. "You, my lady, I have kissed on the lips. I would like to do so again."

"You would?" She didn't know what to do or how to answer. Was he asking her permission or just announcing his upcoming move?

"Unless you would rather I didn't?"

Her heart pounded so loudly she was sure he could hear it too. "I don't mind." With her head downward she looked up at him shyly.

Then his hand moved to her chin and he raised it until they gazed into each other's eyes. He leaned over and ever so gently placed his lips upon hers. Regina's eyes closed and she surrendered to the moment, melting from his touch, craving his kisses, feeling so safe and happy in his embrace.

The kiss lingered for a moment. Part of her wished that he'd touch her more. Instead, he slowly dropped his hand to the side and their mouths parted. Her eyes opened to find him still staring at her, but he had that serious look on his face again.

"I suppose I was addled to do that."

"Why would you say that?" She longed for another kiss but could tell it wasn't going to happen. Something took his concern.

"I am naught but a commoner, Lady Regina." He was back to using her title again which made Regina feel distance between them.

"I know that."

"You are a noblewoman."

"Yes, I am. So what is your point?"

"I have no right to kiss you. Nothing can ever come of this. I am sorry that I put you in such a horrible position when I swam in the lake naked, and I am sorry I was so bold as to kiss you again just now."

"I don't mind," she told him, wanting to say how much she enjoyed it but never having a chance to do so.

He hopped off the end of the cart. "I'll retrieve your shoes before the others return and think we've misbehaved ourselves in the hay."

When he said the words, it only made her want to misbehave in the hay with him even more than ever. He returned with the shoes and held one out, tapping the top of his leg.

"Put your foot here," he told her. "I will help you don your shoes."

She did as instructed, liking the feel of his strong thigh beneath her foot. She also liked the feel of his big hands holding her. What was the matter with her? She had never felt this way about a man before. Then again, no other man had kissed her the way Hunter did, or helped her put on her shoes. She was slowly losing her heart to him and could do nothing to stop it.

"Here come the others," he told her, releasing her and standing up tall. "I think I'll go meet them. I need to get Luke to like me again and not think I want to drown his damned cat."

Her heart went out to him as she watched him approach the others. Sage and Robin each held one of Martin's hands, swinging the little boy between them as they walked. Anyone could see how in love her brother and his wife were. They had a family already and it would be growing by leaps and bounds in a few months' time. Regina had never longed for a husband before or a family either. She'd always been too busy with training her birds to even think or care about falling in love. Since she'd met Hunter, her thoughts were changing now. This change was confusing, exciting, and at the same time draining.

She watched Hunter approach Luke, trying to talk to the boy. He held out his hands for the cat, but Luke clutched her to his chest and ran to the wagon leaving him behind. Luke jumped in next to her, still petting Inky.

"Hello, Luke," said Regina, trying to make conversation. "Did your cat enjoy the walk?"

"Yes," he answered, not bothering to look up. "Did you enjoy your time all alone with my uncle?"

She jerked backward. That took her by surprise. "Yes, we talked and I enjoyed the conversation. Why do you ask?"

"I saw him kiss you from all the way down by the creek." Luke didn't sound happy about it at all.

"Oh," she said, not wanting to deny it. "Luke, does it bother you that your uncle kissed me?" she asked, starting to get an idea of what was bothering the boy.

"I don't care at all," he told her. "I have a new friend now. I don't need Hunter anymore." He stood up and walked across the wagon, distancing himself and huddling down right behind the driver's seat.

Her brother came over and put Martin in the wagon. "He wants to ride with you, Regina," said Robin. "Would you mind holding on to Martin?"

"Of course I don't mind." She took Martin onto her lap.

"Robin, I want to ride in the back with Regina," said Sage. "Can Hunter ride up front with you?"

"I suppose so," said Robin, lifting his wife and helping her get settled. "Just move in from the end so you don't fall out if we hit a bump."

"Robin, I am thankful that you care, but you are being ridiculous. I am not going to get hurt and neither will I injure the babies."

"I'll make sure she doesn't fall out," Regina promised her brother.

"Well, all right." Robin walked over to Hunter and together they went to the driver's seat. In a moment the wagon lurched and they started back to the castle.

"Well? How did it go with Hunter?" asked Sage.

"Oh, so that was your plan, was it?" asked Regina. "Is it also why you wanted to ride in back with me now?"

"Mayhap. Now, do tell."

Regina didn't want to talk about the kiss with Luke in the wagon and Martin on her lap. Everyone seemed to have eyes like a hawk and ears like an owl.

"Everything is fine," she told Sage, her eyes roaming over to Luke who seemed so hurt or dejected. "However, I think I know why someone is acting a certain way to someone else now."

"What?" Sage made a face. "Regina, you are making no sense at all."

"Since when does anything in our lives ever make sense?" asked Regina, feeling as if she were falling for a commoner just like her siblings and so many of her cousins had done as well. It was the last thing in the world that she thought would ever happen to her.

CHAPTER 8

Hunter stood in the ladies solar the next morning while Regina's Uncle William measured Luke to make him noble clothing.

"Can I go now?" Luke said with a puff of air from his mouth. "Fred is going to introduce me to his friends today. They all want to meet Inky."

"Yes, go," said Hunter, not wanting a confrontation with the boy in front of so many people. Lady Sage as well as the ladies Penelope and Jean were stitching. The old woman Lady Gertrude was there as well, smiling and winking at him every time he looked her way.

"Come on, Inky," said Luke, pulling the cat out of William's sewing box where she was tangled up in all the thread. Luke held the cat up to his face and gave her a quick kiss. Damn, the boy was getting too attached to the animal and it was going to be harder than ever for Hunter to tell Luke he couldn't keep the cat.

"That sure looks like my missing cat," said William, eyeing up the animal. "She has been missing for a few days now. Where did you get her?"

Luke pulled Inky closer to his chest and frowned. "She is my cat," he answered. "Fred and I found her in the stables and she's a stray." He then took the cat and darted to the door, leaving as quickly as possible.

"Why would you think that is your cat, William?" asked Hunter as William started measuring him next. "After all, you live in town and Luke found her here at the castle."

"I know," said William. "But my daughter gave us a cat to help catch mice around the shop. It was black with a small white spot on her front left paw. Just like the cat Luke has."

Hunter got a bad feeling in his gut hearing this. Luke had been acting odd lately. It was a little suspicious that the boy had been saying he wanted a black cat and suddenly as soon as they got here he found a stray one. Still, Hunter needed to give his nephew the benefit of the doubt.

"I suppose it is just a coincidence," said Hunter. "After all, a lot of cats look alike."

"I suppose," said William. "However, it is odd that both cats would have a white spot on their paw."

"I've seen crazier things than that." Hunter realized it was strange indeed. Still, he needed to trust Luke.

"I have a tunic here that I think will fit you. Take off yours and try it on." William held up a gray tunic with ornate embroidery around the sleeves. It was obviously made for a nobleman.

"Sure," said Hunter, reaching behind his neck and pulling his tunic up and over his head. He thought he heard a gasp and then a giggle. He looked back to the women and they were all on the edge of their chairs gawking at him. "Oh, great," he mumbled.

Just then the door to the solar opened and in walked Regina. She carried a basket of stitching. She stopped when she saw Hunter's bare chest and all the ladies gawking at him. Her mouth dropped open and her basket fell to the floor, sending the contents scattering everywhere.

"I'll get that, Lady Regina." Hunter dashed across the room, hunkering down at Regina's feet. He quickly scooped up the thread, cloth and needles and stuffed everything back into the sewing basket. Standing back up, he held it out to her. "Here you are, my lady. I hope nothing was ruined."

Hunter noticed her looking behind him.Turning his head slightly he saw all the ladies watching his every move. Suddenly, he felt very naked. He also realized the only thing that might have been ruined was Regina's reputation since he'd run to her side to help her. Once again, being half naked. Already kicking himself for his mistake, he shoved the basket into Regina's hands and spun around, hurrying back to William.

"Give me that," Hunter told William, snatching the tunic away from the man and hurriedly pulling it over his head.

"Hold still, I need to alter it." William stuck a pin between his lips while his lithe fingers pulled at the tunic in a few places. Heat engulfed Hunter since he knew without having to even turn around that every one of the ladies was staring at him. "All right, that should do it," said William, placing the last pin. It should be good now as soon as I make a few adjustments. Take it off."

"Really," Hunter muttered, cringing at the thought but did so anyway.

"I need to measure you for a pair of breeches now." William brought his measuring string over to Hunter. The man got down on his knees at Hunter's feet. Then he reached out and put one end of the string at Hunter's waist and let it trail down to his foot. "All right. Now I need to measure the length to the crotch."

"Nay! That's good enough." Hunter grasped his own tunic, pulling it quickly over his head. When he turned around Regina was standing there with her arms crossed.

"Why are you doing that here in the ladies solar?" she asked. "You should be elsewhere. This room is for ladies. To sew."

"I'm afraid that is my fault," William spoke up. "I thought it would be easier to just measure Hunter and the boy here since this is where I'll be constructing their garments during my stay."

There came a few more giggles from behind them. William looked up, realizing this was a huge mistake. "I'm so sorry, my lady."

"Do your measuring in the privacy of Hunter's chamber from now on please," said Regina with a stiff upper lip.

"I think I've got more than enough measurements." William busied himself, fussing with things in his sewing box.

"Good, because I'm here to tell Hunter that his presence is needed in the mews at once."

"It is?" This confused Hunter. "Why?" he asked. "I thought I wasn't to have any more training with the birds."

"Well, I've decided differently," said Regina. "Now put

your boots back on and follow me please. It is getting late and there is much to do."

"Of course, my lady." Hunter didn't understand what was going on, but decided just to follow orders and not even ask right now. He shoved his feet back into his boots.

"I will have your garments as well as the boy's ready for you later today," William called out to him. "You can try them on in your chamber later for a last fitting."

"Thank you," said Hunter, whisking past the ladies, following Regina to the door. When he got in front of Lady Gertrude, he felt a sharp prick on his behind. "Ouch!" He jumped and held his hand to his buttocks. Turning around, he saw all three ladies looking like lionesses on the hunt, wanting to eat him.

"Oops. So sorry about that, Lord Hunter," said Lady Gertrude. "I lost control of my needle." She held up the needle and grinned.

"Ladies, back to work," called out Sage. "Please leave Lord Hunter alone."

"Yes, please do," he mumbled hurrying out the door and pulling it closed behind him.

Regina stood there trying to hold back a laugh if he wasn't mistaken.

"Those ladies are hyenas," he told her, still rubbing the sting on his ass.

"Well, what did you expect? They've all heard that you like to be naked and wanted to see more. I am sure they enjoyed the show you put on for them."

He groaned again. "Well, I promise that from now on the only woman I get naked in front of is you."

It was his turn to hold back his laughter as he walked away leaving Regina with her mouth hanging open.

"Well, why did you call me here?" asked Hunter, following Regina into the mews. "It sounded important."

"It is," she said, looking around the mews and calling out. "Cassian? Roger? Are you here?" When there came no answer, she released the breath she'd been holding. Thankfully, neither Cassian or Roger were here at the moment and that was exactly what she wanted. She needed to be alone with Hunter to tell him she had feelings for him. This was her perfect opportunity to do so.

"Go on," he said.

She turned to face him. "I wanted to add to our conversation from yesterday."

"Our...conversation?"

"Yes. The one we had while on our outing."

"Add to it? I don't understand. What does that mean?"

"You said you had feelings for me."

"Oh, that. I'd rather not revisit that conversation again, my lady, since we both know it is naught but a dead end."

She wanted to tell him that it wasn't a dead end. That she reciprocated the feelings too. She wanted to tell him that she didn't care that he was a commoner because she had never felt so strongly attracted to any man before in her life. But then her thoughts seemed to get muddled in her head. Her tongue suddenly felt three sizes too big for her mouth. Regina was about to express her affection to a man she barely knew and it was making her so hot and heady that she wanted to rip her clothes off just to cool down and not combust.

"Oh, here comes Roger now across the courtyard," he said, stretching his neck to see out the door from their position in the mews.

"What?" She looked up to see it was true. Damn. This isn't at all what she wanted. If Roger came in now, she couldn't express her affection for Hunter. She wasn't sure when she'd have another opportunity to do so. Panicked, she grabbed Hunter's arm and spun him around, doing the only thing she could think of that would get her message across quickly. She reached up and kissed Hunter hard on the mouth.

"Mmmph," mumbled Hunter, taken by surprise. His hands went around her waist and he pulled her closer, reciprocating by kissing her back. "Mmmmm," he moaned in pleasure.

Regina could see the door of the mews from the corner of her eyes. Roger was quickly approaching. She shoved Hunter's hands away and stepped back with a jerk.

"Huh? What was that all about?" he asked, blinking in confusion. "And why did you pull away?"

"I wanted to tell you that I have feelings for you as well," she said hurriedly and in a soft voice. "But I didn't have time to say it so I just kissed you, not knowing if we'd ever be alone again."

"Regina, really?" he asked, sounding pleased by her confession.

"Yes, but don't say another word about it. And be sure not to stand too close to me. Here comes Roger now."

. . .

Hunter's mind soared. Whenever he was around Regina he had no idea what to expect with her. A kiss sometimes. A slap at other times. And now a confession of attraction that was instantly followed by a threat to stay silent about it. She was a complicated woman and one he wasn't sure he would ever understand.

"Good morning, Roger," called out Regina, waving to the boy as he entered the mews.

"Good morning, everyone," Roger answered with a quick wave back. "It is going to be a beautiful day."

That's when Hunter spotted someone standing in the shadows with their back toward them. He nodded to Regina and used his eyes to point the man out, realizing it was Cassian inside the mews.

Regina looked over her shoulder and then back at Hunter.

"I think he was here all the time," he whispered.

"It doesn't matter. He can't hear a thing," Regina told Hunter with a dismissing swish of her hand through the air.

"What did you want me to do today, Lady Regina?" asked Roger. "The usual?"

"Actually, I've decided I want to go on a hunting trip tomorrow," Regina answered.

"Hunting? You? With the birds?" asked Hunter.

"Yes, me. However, I'll only be taking Hera. She hasn't been hunting in a while and needs the exercise as well as the practice," Regina explained.

"Aye, my lady. I will ready things for the trip," said Roger. "Will I be joining you?"

"Nay. I'll need you to stay here with the rest of the birds."

"If I come along we can bring two of the birds. They can hunt in a pair the way we've been practicing with them," suggested Roger. "Cassian will be here to take care of the rest."

Regina nodded in agreement. "You're right, Roger. That is important. Can you please find Lord Robin for me? Tell him the birds need to hunt and that I'd like him to organize a hunting party for tomorrow."

"Yes, my lady," said Roger, hurrying out the door.

"You give orders to your brother?" asked Hunter in surprise.

"Only when it comes to hunting with the birds. He knows that I know the best times to take them. There are certain times when the birds are molting that they won't be able to hunt at all."

"I am guessing this isn't molting season yet?"

"Not yet, so we are fine."

"Oh, my lord, my lady, I didn't know you were here," came Cassian's voice from across the mews.

"Cassian, I need you to go to the kitchen and have the cook fill the food bag for the birds, please. I want to start training right away."

"Of course, my lady." Cassian started to shuffle toward the door.

"Don't forget the bag," called out Regina but the man was already past them and couldn't hear them.

"I'll take it to him." Hunter picked up the empty food bag and raced after Cassian. He was just about up to him when Cassian turned around with his hand outstretched.

Hunter stopped in his tracks, handing him the bag. It was almost as if he'd heard him coming, although that couldn't be true since the man could barely hear.

"I know I've seen you before." Cassian looked Hunter up and down. "You are hiding something, and I am going to figure out just what it is." Cassian turned and headed out the door.

"What did he say?" Regina came to join him.

"Nothing of importance."

"Hunter, I just realized that I never introduced you to all my birds and neither have I showed you around the mews."

"Nay, you haven't."

"Follow me." Regina took his hand in hers and led him over to the perches where the birds sat silently with hoods over their eyes. He liked the feel of holding her hand. Hunter also liked that no one else was around or she probably wouldn't have done it.

"Is it really necessary to cover their eyes with those leather hoods?" asked Hunter. The birds wore hoods that looked so silly in his opinion. Most of the coverings had ornate designs on them and ridiculous long plumage atop the head.

"As I told you before, it is. These birds are easily startled. They can also see things moving from far distances and it distracts them. The hoods over their eyes keep them calm and rested."

"How many birds do you house in the mews?" Hunter raised his head and looked around.

"Right now we have only four birds of prey living here. However, I am going to talk Robin into getting more soon."

"Talk him into it? So he doesn't want more birds then?"

"My brother doesn't yet realize the importance of a good bird of prey. Once his larder is always filled to the brim and it lasts throughout the winter, he'll be thanking me."

"I suppose that makes sense."

"This is my smallest bird, Dewdrop," she said, showing him a colorful bird with orange and gray plumage. "She is a kestrel," explained Regina.

"I see."

"This one is my goshawk, Cloud. He is a young bird yet and is still in training but learning quickly." She showed him a larger bird than the first with brown and black on its wings. It had streaked tones on its belly.

"Hello, Cloud," he said, reaching out to touch it but she grabbed his hand and stopped him.

"Don't do that! I thought I already warned you not to try to touch the birds. Even though they are wearing hoods and cannot see you, they can still bite. Keep your hands to yourself."

"Right," he said with a nod, pulling his hand back. "I suppose they have sharp beaks."

"Sharp enough to tear the flesh off their prey in midflight. Plus their talons are like knife blades too."

"I'll keep my fingers intact, thank you." Hunter clasped his hands behind his back as they walked to the next perch.

"This is Lightning, my peregrine falcon. You already met her the other night at the lake."

"Yes. I'm sure Lightning remembers me as being the crazy naked man in the water."

That made her giggle. "The last bird is my oldest, my largest, and also my favorite. Hunter, meet Hera, my gyrfalcon. She is eight years old."

The bird had a lot of white on her, especially on her chest. Hera's feathers on her back and wings were of a grayish brown. Her feet were yellow and her beak had a blue tint. She was truly a beautiful bird.

"Yes, she certainly is a lot bigger than the others," surmised Hunter.

"The gyrfalcon is the largest falcon that exists, while the peregrine is the fastest," Regina explained.

"Isn't eight years an old age for a bird?" He was truly curious about the birds and wanted to learn more.

"In the wild, yes, it is. Ten is usually their lifespan. However, birds in captivity live a lot longer. I heard from another falconer that he knew of a gyrfalcon that lived to be thirty under a rich lord's care. I hope Hera lives at least that long."

"Yes. Me, too," said Hunter.

Regina took the falconer's leather glove and slipped it onto her left hand. Then she used her right hand to untie Hera's straps that were keeping her on the perch. "These leather straps on the birds' legs are called jesses," she explained. "There are sometimes little bells attached to the bottom, but I only put them on some of the birds. Hera doesn't wear them."

"Bells? Whatever for?"

"It comes in handy if the bird goes after prey and loses sight of its master. Sometimes the bird will fly too far and get lost. Listening for the bells helps us to locate them."

"This is all interesting knowledge."

"There is a lot involved in falconry. For instance, you must remember at all times that even though the birds can recognize a trainer's voice or face, they are still birds of prey.

So one must always be on their guard."

"Do all of these birds hunt and kill the same type of prey?" he asked, honestly interested in falconry now, and not just the falconer.

"Shortwings like goshawks or kestrels usually hunt ground prey like rabbits or pheasant," she told him. "Those birds like to sit and watch from trees."

"What about birds like Hera?" he asked.

"Longwing birds such as peregrine falcons or gyrfalcons hunt in the air and normally catch birds in midflight. They are extremely good in open areas and moorlands whereas birds like Cloud do better in wooded areas."

"So which birds will be going on the hunt tomorrow?"

"Tomorrow, I'll be taking Hera and Lightning with us. I have been working with Roger to train them to hunt in pairs and it has been working."

"In pairs? Really? Even though they are different species?"

"It isn't common, but can be done. Actually, the hunting dogs know how to hunt with the birds of prey as well. They work well together."

"The dogs? They hunt along with the birds? How?"

"Easy," she answered. "The hounds scare the prey out into the open and the birds catch it."

"Regina, you are amazing."

"What do you mean?" She removed the hood from Hera and took the bird onto her glove, wrapping the jesses tightly around her hand.

"I have never known a woman who is so confident and good at things the way you are. Especially something that takes true skill like falconry."

"Thank you." She flashed him a quick smile, still looking at her bird. "It's because I have true passion for what I do."

"Yes," he said, thinking of the passion she showed in her kissing. "I believe you do everything with passion."

"Well, why not? With passion and lots of practice comes skill and perfection. Don't you think?" She looked at him directly, her cute little mouth turning up like a bow.

"I would like to practice that passion with you while I use my skills," he told her, staring at her mouth. "I am sure that together we can find true perfection."

He was talking about making love to her and he was sure she knew it. But instead of responding, she did probably what any good falconer would do. She changed the subject and talked about the birds.

"I think it is time Hera gets to know you. Give me your hand." She held out her free hand to him, still balancing the bird on the other.

"What?" That took him by surprise. "How are we going to do that?"

"Hera, this is Hunter," she spoke to the bird. "Don't worry, he doesn't hunt birds like you so you don't need to fear him." She spoke in a soft and calming voice. Regina put her hand over his and gently reached up and ran his fingers over the bird's back.

Excitement coursed through him. Not only from the fact he was actually touching the bird and not getting his fingers bit off, but because Regina was holding his hand again and this time it was different. Something happened today between them that was truly important.

That 'something' was that Regina trusted him, and this proved it. He never thought for a minute this would really happen even though he had always hoped it would. She trusted him enough to let him touch her bird! She was even telling the bird to trust him as well.

Damn, this was a good feeling. It was something that he would never forget as long as he lived.

CHAPTER 9

"Luke, I am going on a hunting expedition today and I want you to join me." Hunter decided he needed to spend more time with his nephew if the boy was ever going to start listening to him.

"Why?" Luke played with Inky atop the bed in their chamber. "Isn't it bad enough I have to wear these silly clothes?" William had dropped off clothes for both of them yesterday and Hunter had to fight with Luke to even put them on this morning.

"These are the clothes of nobles. You should be happy to wear them since you always said you wanted to be a knight."

"I've changed my mind," Luke told him. "I want to be a stableboy instead."

"Fred again, huh?" Hunter pulled his new tunic over his head. It seemed to fit well but wasn't as comfortable as his old clothes. He couldn't blame the boy for not wanting to change the way they dressed.

"If I wear these clothes around Fred, he is going to feel poor." Luke sounded as if he actually cared about his friend's feelings. This was something new since Luke had never acted this way before.

"Fred is a stableboy, Luke. He's not supposed to feel rich." Hunter sat on the bed and pulled up the new breeches that William had made him. They fit like a glove and that impressed him. Regina's uncle truly was a master at his skill.

"Well, I'm not supposed to be rich either so why do I have to dress this way?"

"You are posing as a noble. Fred doesn't know you really aren't so you need to keep up appearances."

"Nay, he doesn't." Luke got off the bed holding the cat. He'd been feeding it so much that the cat was getting a fat belly.

"What does that mean?" asked Hunter.

"I told Fred I'm a thief-taker just like you."

"You did what?" In anger, Hunter jumped up, managing to scare the cat. Inky jumped out of Luke's arms and bolted across the room. The door opened just then and the cat slipped out, disappearing down the corridor.

"Inky got away! I need to catch him." Luke rushed out the door, knocking into William who was entering with his sewing basket under his arm.

"My lord? I knocked but I guess you didn't hear me. I came for a final fitting," said William.

"My clothes fit fine, William, thank you. Your services won't be needed today."

William looked out the door and then entered the room, closing the door behind him. "May I have a word with you in private, my lord?"

"Yes, of course." Hunter bent down and put on his boots. He thought it was odd that William called him a lord when he knew damned well that Hunter wasn't noble. He supposed it was because William was keeping up the guise and he was thankful that the man was going along with it. "What's on your mind, William?"

"I wouldn't even mention it, but since Robin is having trouble with thieves lately, I feel it is my duty to do so."

"Mention what? What are you talking about?" Hunter walked across the room to a small table that held some of his personal things.

"It's about that cat that Luke has, my lord. I got a better look at her just now and I am sure she is the same one that disappeared from my shop."

Hunter looked up, not knowing what to say. "Do you really think so?"

"Yes. I'm sure of it."

"I see." Hunter reached down to the table and picked up his boar-bristle brush. "Well, mayhap she got out and wandered away and Luke found her." Hunter ran the brush through his tangled long hair.

"Aye, I supposed you're right," William answered with his head down.

Hunter looked over at William and slowly put down the brush. "You think my nephew is a thief, don't you?"

"Nay, my lord, I didn't say that." William's eyes opened wide and he shook his head. "However, there is something else I think you should know."

"What's that?"

William squirmed, seeming really uncomfortable. "It doesn't matter. I'm sure it is nothing."

"It sounds important, William. I think you should tell me."

"If you insist." He still squirmed, moving his sewing basket from one arm to the other.

"I insist. Now please, tell me. What has taken your concern?"

William ran a hand over his basket and let out a deep sigh before continuing. "Right before my cat disappeared, my daughter said two boys were hanging out in front of the shop in a suspicious manner."

"Really." Hunter didn't want to hear this. "William, if my nephew has done anything wrong, I swear I will punish him and correct the situation. If he has your cat, as you say, I will make sure she is returned to you."

"Nay, nay." William raised his hand in the air. "I don't want the cat back. I can get another. I just noticed that your relations with your nephew seem a little...shall I say, rocky?"

Hunter blew out a deep breath and collapsed atop the bed. "Mayhap stormy is a better word to describe it. It is like I don't even know who the boy is anymore. Please tell me that raising a child gets easier because this isn't going well at all."

"I can't say it does, unfortunately. Then again, Bernadette and I had girls, not a boy. I'm sure it is much different."

"William, you are easy to talk to. I feel comfortable around you."

"Thank you," said the man, slowly lowering himself atop a chair. "Does that mean there is something you need to discuss but can't find the right person to talk to about it?"

"You are a wise man as well," said Hunter with a smile, sitting up on the bed. "It's about Lady Regina."

"Ah, I thought so." The man put his sewing basket on his lap and chuckled. "You have feelings for her but you can't tell Robin because you are a commoner and she is his brother. Is that right?"

"Damn, you are good at this. How did you know that?"

"I grew up in a much different lifestyle than Robin, you realize. It was more like yours I'd guess. I may be good at my craft, but I don't have book knowledge. I learned all that I know on the streets."

"Is it hard having a brother who is now a noble?"

"We're not really brothers," he said. "But the answer is no. I felt as if Madoc were my true brother even though he wasn't. I know it is proper to treat nobles differently, but honestly, they are no different from commoners in my opinion. They just have a title attached to their name."

"Not to mention a lot of wealth and status."

"Have you told Regina your feelings for her?"

"I have."

"How did she react?"

"Lady Regina is...complicated."

"She is, indeed!"

Hunter and William both chuckled.

"I didn't think she cared for me at first," admitted Hunter. "Then things changed recently and now I think that mayhap she does. I might just be fooling myself though. We don't belong together, and I know it. I am sure nothing will ever come of any feelings that we have for each other."

"Don't give up hope, Hunter. If you want something...or

someone bad enough, there is always a way to get what you want."

"That's just it. I'm not really sure where I want our relationship to go." Now Hunter was the one fidgeting and feeling uncomfortable. He didn't know William well but was opening up to him about his personal feelings. Mayhap he shouldn't be talking to him. After all, William was Madoc's brother and Madoc was Regina's father. His mind became even more confused.

"So, are you saying you don't want to get married and settle down and have a family someday?" asked William.

"Nay, I'm not saying that at all. I am just saying that I'm not sure I'd be any good at it. I don't have any admirable skills like you do with sewing or like Regina does with falconry. How could she ever be proud of me?"

"Leave that up to her to decide," was William's wise advice. "Don't you have some kind of skill you are proud of? I mean, you are a thief-taker, right?"

"Phiff," he said, blowing air from his mouth. "I don't think any woman, noble or not, would brag about her husband being nothing more than a blasted bounty hunter."

"Then what did you do before you were a thief-taker?" asked William. "Mayhap that is what you should focus on."

"Nay. Never."

"What do you mean?"

"As a boy, the same age as Luke, I traveled with my father. As mercenaries."

"Oh." William made a face. "I see what you mean. But at least you are a fighting man. That is a skill well admired."

"Mayhap if you're a knight, which I'll never be. Otherwise, I'm just considered a killer. I have been born lowly and some things are just out of my reach, I'm afraid."

"Find the thief," said William. "You do that and you will make a lot of nobles happy, and shine in Regina's eyes as well. Do what you're good at, and let the rest fall in place as it will."

"Oh, I will find the thief, I promise you that. It is only a matter of time." Hunter had faith in his abilities and this didn't worry him at all. "However, I must admit that I am not really in a big hurry to do so."

"You're not?" William seemed confused. "I don't understand. Why not?"

"Because, William, as soon as I find and deliver the thief, I will have to leave Shrewsbury Castle and go back to my old life. My life, that is, without Lady Regina."

Regina sat atop her horse with Hera on her arm, waiting for Hunter outside the stable. The hunting party which consisted of Robin, his squire, and two huntsmen were all packed and ready to leave. Abe, the kennelgroom was also there with two of the hunting dogs on leads.

"Are we ready to go?" Robin asked her, giving his wife Sage a hug and kiss goodbye.

"We are still waiting for Hunter and Luke," she told him. "Oh, here comes Hunter now."

Hunter arrived and the stable groom, Al brought his horse as well as Luke's to him.

"Lord Hunter," said Regina from atop her horse. "I'd like you to meet Lord Robin's squire, Baldwin. Also the kennelgroom, Abe, and two of our huntsmen, Gregory and Paul."

"Hello, happy to meet you," said Hunter with a quick nod. "I am sorry I am late but I've been looking for my nephew, Luke. Have any of you seen him?"

Regina looked up to see Luke hobbling toward him from the keep. "There he is," she said with a nod.

"Luke, hurry up," growled Hunter. "You are making everyone wait."

"I can't go on the hunt today," said the boy. "I fell down the stairs to the battlements and hurt my leg." Luke bent down and rubbed his leg.

"Oh, you poor thing," said Sage, hurrying over to him. "Let me see it. I am a healer."

When Luke showed her his leg, Regina noticed that the boy was wearing boots that were several sizes too big for him. "Mayhap he tripped because his boots are too big," she pointed out.

Hunter looked down at the boy's feet. "Luke? Where did you get those boots? And what the hell were you doing up on the battlements? You don't belong up there." Hunter's tone was filled with anger making Regina sure that he was about to reprimand the boy.

"Hunter, Hera is getting restless and it is time to go," she called out, not wanting a confrontation right before they left. Especially not in front of everyone.

"Get on your horse, Luke. Now," commanded Hunter, mounting his steed.

"Oh, nay, he can't mount a horse let alone go anywhere," said Sage, inspecting his leg. "His knee is scraped and bleeding and also bruised. His ankle is also starting to swell.

Leave him here with me and I will apply a healing salve to it. He should be fine by the time you return."

"Yes, I need to stay here, Hunter," said the boy, getting a look that could kill from Hunter.

"We'll discuss this when I return," Hunter told him. "Now, stay out of trouble, and I mean it."

"I'll watch over him," offered Sage, being the kind woman and excellent mother that she was. Sage was used to being around children since her parents had died when she was young and it had been up to her to raise her siblings.

Fred appeared from the stables with Inky in his arms. He put the cat down on the ground and she ran over to Luke, rubbing against his leg. Luke sat right down on the ground and put the cat on his lap.

Hunter rode over to Regina. "Where is Roger?" he asked. "I thought he was going to bring Cloud along on the hunt too."

"It was Lightning we planned to bring," she corrected him. "Unfortunately, that plan has changed."

"Really? Why?"

"Roger is ill today," she told him. "He stayed in the village this morning with his family. It seems he must have eaten something that didn't agree with him yesterday."

"I see. So, who is going to watch over the other birds then?" asked Hunter.

Regina looked up to see Cassian standing in the doorway of the mews watching them. "Cassian will be here to look after them," she said, getting a bad feeling about leaving the care of the birds to the man.

"You don't sound as if you like that idea," commented Hunter.

Regina let out a deep breath and looked over to Hera on her arm. "I wish I could bring all my birds with me today, but since I cannot, I suggest we leave for the hunt."

One of the huntsmen blew a horn to announce their departure. Robin led the way with his squire and the huntsmen rode right behind him. The kennelgroom was on foot, with the hounds pulling him as he held onto their leads.

"Is the kennelgroom going to run the whole way?" asked Hunter in disbelief, feeling sorry for the poor man. He almost wanted to offer Abe a ride atop his horse.

"Yes, he will run. He needs to do so, in order to control the dogs," explained Regina. "Don't worry about Abe. We don't ride very fast. He'll be able to keep up with us."

"If you say so." Hunter looked at the land, liking the feeling of being in nature. The sky was so blue and wide. The trees were turning green quickly, and even some of the flowers were already blooming, filling the air with a sweet scent. The castle was nice, but it felt so confining and crowded to him. He wasn't used to always being around so many people. Part of him longed to get back to his home in the woods. "I'm sorry about that scene with Luke earlier." Hunter rode up beside Regina. "I will reprimand the boy and get to the bottom of things when we return."

"He does seem to be a handful," said Regina, reaching over to give Hera a treat as they rode.

"I thought William could give me some pointers on parenting, but since he has girls, he wasn't much help." Hunter wasn't sure why he told this information to Regina because it probably only made him seem week. But he was searching for things to talk about because he liked being with Regina and wanted to spend as much time with her as possible before he had to leave.

"You saw my Uncle William?" she asked, sounding surprised.

"Yes," he answered. "William stopped by my chamber this morning to make sure my clothes fit right and we talked."

"What else did you talk about?" she asked curiously.

"Just...things," he said, quickly looking the other way.

Regina smiled. She had a feeling Hunter had been talking about her to William and she couldn't say it displeased her. Now, she only wished she knew exactly what had been said.

CHAPTER 10

"I have never seen anything so beautiful in my entire life," said Hunter later that day, looking at Regina even though he was sure she thought he was talking about her bird. He watched Hera take off from Regina's glove, lifting up into the sky. The bright white plumage of the bird almost seemed to glow in the sun. The falcon flew so fast that it didn't take long for her to almost seem to disappear in the sky.

"Yes, it is a wonderful feeling as well as frightening," stated Regina, digging into the pouch hanging at her side for a piece of raw meat for the bird.

"What do you mean?" asked Hunter.

"My heart speeds up every time one of my birds takes off in flight. I know they are trained to return, but there is always a sickening feeling in the pit of my stomach that they might just like being free and not want to come back."

"Has that ever happened?" Hunter watched the bird

loop around above the lake and start heading back toward Regina.

"Nay. Not yet, anyway. And I hope it never will." Regina whistled for the bird and held up her arm, letting Hera know it was time to return.

Hera swept through the sky, landing expertly on the falconer's glove. Regina quickly rewarded the bird with a scrap of raw meat.

"What kind of meat is that you are feeding the bird?" he asked.

"Usually whatever the kitchen has. Chicken, rabbit, or even rodents. The birds love pigeon but of course I am not allowed to give them any since my father has his carrier pigeons at the castle. He gets very upset if the cook even suggests making a pigeon stew."

"Regina, the hounds are ready and the hunters have spotted ducks on the water," Robin called out to her. "Is the falcon ready too?"

"Yes, Hera is ready as well," she answered back.

"What happens now?" asked Hunter.

"The kennelgroom will take the hounds down to the water where they will flush out the ducks. The water fowl will fly up into the sky and Hera will hunt and bring what she catches back to me. The same thing will happen as soon as the hunters spot grouse in the bushes later on when we hunt ground prey."

"So the bird can hunt in flight and catch game on the ground both?" Hunter wanted to learn as much as he could about these interesting birds.

"Yes," she answered with a nod. Then she looked over at

her bird. "Are you ready, Hera?" Raising her arm in the air, the falcon flapped her wings and took off in flight.

Hunter heard the hounds barking down at the water and then the sound of many beating wings against air as a flush of ducks took off in flight. Hera was truly amazing. Flying above the flock, she dove down, catching one in midflight, clutching it with her talons. Then she flew back to Regina.

"Watch out," shouted Regina, running toward the water probably so the bird wouldn't have to fly as far with the heavy duck in her talons. Hera landed at Regina's feet with the duck still in her grip. "Good girl, Hera." Regina put the raw meat in front of the bird to lure her back to her glove, getting the falcon to drop the prey. One of the huntsmen scooped up the duck and took it away.

"That was fantastic! Just amazing beyond words." Hunter joined her, beaming with pride, almost as if the bird were his. "You should be proud of what you've trained this bird to do," he told Regina.

"I am proud of each of my birds as if they were my own children. I don't know what I'd ever do without them."

The day went by fast and before Regina knew it, the sun was already setting. They had made camp for the night and were sitting around the fire eating roasted duck, compliments of Hera. The hunt today, with the help of the falcon and also the hounds had been successful. They managed to bag a dozen ducks, six rabbits, four pheasants and even a lone badger. Regina was tired and she knew that Hera was probably exhausted. The falcon had more exercise today than she'd had in a long time.

"So, Hunter, what did you think of the hunt?" asked Robin, raising a cup of wine to drink. The night was still and the hounds had been rewarded with a rabbit each for their meal. Robin's squire had cooked meat for them all and the huntsmen had helped to set up camp. There were three tents. One for Robin and his squire, another for the huntsmen, the kennelgroom and the dogs, and the last for Lady Regina.

"It was an experience of a lifetime that I'll never forget," Hunter answered. "I've never seen anything so beautiful in my life."

Regina looked over to realize Hunter was staring at her when he said that. Did he mean she was beautiful? Somehow, she thought so. She was sure the others must have realized it too and would see the blush rising quickly to her cheeks.

"It's too bad we didn't have two birds as was planned," said Robin. "We could have brought in twice as much game."

"Yes, I hope Roger is all right," said Regina. "I wonder what he ate that disagreed with him so violently."

"I was sitting with him last night at the meal," Baldwin spoke up. "I ate the exact same food as he did, yet I feel fine."

"Us too," agreed Paul. "It doesn't make any sense."

"Nay, it doesn't," agreed the second huntsmen, Gregory. "Especially since Roger has always had a stomach that could withstand anything. I swear if he ate poison, it still wouldn't bother him."

"Poison?" Hunter stopped eating and looked up. "Tell me, who else sat with Roger for the meal last night?"

"Just the usual," said the kennelgroom, brushing his dogs. "You know, me, Gregory, Paul, Baldwin, the stable groom and his grandson, and the old deaf man from the mews."

"Do you mean Cassian?" Hunter seemed extremely interested in this bit of information.

"Aye, that oddball," said Paul. "He couldn't even hear that nephew of yours when the boy was bragging how he won a pair of boots off a castle guard in a card game."

"Luke was playing cards?" asked Hunter in surprise. Regina could see the tension building up in the man's face.

"Aye. The boy is damned good at it, too," said the kennelgroom, chewing as he spoke. "After he bled the rest of us dry, he headed up to the battlements to cheat the guards out of their share." He licked the grease from the rabbit off his fingers.

"So that's why he was up on the battlements in the first place," mumbled Hunter. Then under his breath Regina heard him mumble to himself. "I never should have taught him how to gamble."

"My guards were playing cards with a boy?" Robin's temper raised now as well. "I'll see that it is stopped immediately when we return."

"Excuse me, Abe," Hunter said with finger in the air. "Did you say that Luke cheated?"

Abe looked over at the huntsmen and they exchanged quick glances before he focused back on his hounds and started petting them. "Did I say that he cheated?"

"Yes," answered Hunter. "You said after he bled the rest

of you dry, he headed up to the battlements to cheat the castle guards out of their share."

"I'm sorry, I didn't mean that. I guess I was just upset because the boy is so good at what he does."

"Yes. I'm sure he is," grunted Hunter.

Regina decided to intervene to keep the mood uplifting. It had been a good day and she didn't want any arguments or heated discussion ruining the night. Especially since Luke wasn't even here to defend himself. "I think Hera deserves a taste of her kill today. Hunter, please pass me some of that duck."

Hunter handed her some cooked duck off his plate. She giggled because he really didn't know a thing when it came to falconry.

"What's the matter?" he asked, looking down to the duck in his hand.

"Nay, not the cooked meat," she explained."Falcons eat it raw."

"Oh, sorry." Hunter looked around. "Did you want me to cut up a duck for her?"

"I'll get it," said the squire, heading over to the horses that held the kills from the day dangling from ropes. He returned with a whole duck and handed it to Regina.

"The whole thing?" asked Hunter in confusion. "Isn't that a lot?"

"Hera will take what she wants." Regina had a perch set up next to her. She took Hera down off the perch and placed her atop a log and put the dead duck in front of her. Hera used her beak to pluck out the feathers and to pull at the meat as she devoured the prey.

"I thought you were always careful not to feed her too

much," said Hunter. "Didn't you say that you always wanted her to stay hungry so she'd return to the hand that feeds her?"

"Yes, that is true. But since we won't be hunting tomorrow and Hera will have a day of rest, it doesn't matter."

"Aren't you afraid she'll fly away during the night?"

"Nay. She'll be in the tent with me," said Regina. "I have a perch set up in there and I will keep an eye on her."

"Oh, that reminds me, Hunter." Robin yawned before continuing. "I hope you don't mind sleeping out here tonight. We need someone to tend to the fire and watch the horses so no wild animals try to steal our kills." Robin yawned once again.

"Nay. I don't mind," he said, acting as if didn't bother him in the least. Regina wondered if a man like him often slept in the outdoors under the open sky.

The men left one by one to retire to their tents for the evening. That left Hunter and Regina sitting around the fire together with no one else around but the bird. Hera had finished her meal and Regina had put on the bird's hood and had her on the perch next to her again.

"Thank you for inviting me to join in on the hunt today," said Hunter, breaking up twigs and throwing them into the fire. "I learned a lot."

"Thank you for coming," she answered. "So you weren't too bored, then?"

"Bored?" He turned to look at her. "Never." He brushed off his hands and scooted closer to her on the log that they shared. "You are amazing, Regina. I have never known anyone like you."

"You aren't so bad yourself." She liked being with Hunter and would be sad when this all ended and he left the castle for good. "Hunter, what will you do once you apprehend the thief? Where will you go?"

"Back to my cabin in the woods, I guess. Back to catching thieves and trying to figure out how to raise a thirteen-year-old stubborn, defiant boy without going crazy in the meantime."

"Mayhap Luke needs a mother's guiding hand," suggested Regina.

His head jerked upward and his eyes closed partially. "What are you saying?"

"I'm just saying that mayhap it is time you got married."

"You think so?"

"It might help. Don't you have a sweetheart? Someone you could ask to settle down with you?"

She was playing with fire and hoped she wouldn't get burned. It was her way of putting the idea in his head that mayhap he needed to be around a woman more. Settle down. Start a family.

"Now that you mention it, I do have a woman who I'd like to consider my sweetheart."

"You do?" That surprised her. Did he have a woman back home that he'd never told her about? She hoped not.

"Yes, I do. And I would even consider marrying her but I would never ask because I don't think she'd want me as her husband."

"Hunter, don't say that. Have more confidence in yourself. You are an exciting, wonderful man. You'd make a good husband for any girl who was lucky enough to get you."

"Nay. Not any girl," he said, sounding suddenly sad. It

made her wonder if perhaps he had his eye on a woman who didn't want him the way he wanted her.

Suddenly feeling ill that she'd even asked about it, Regina realized it would be best to go to sleep. "I must take Hera to her perch in the tent now. She's had a big day and is tired." Regina stood up and took the bird onto her glove.

"Allow me to escort you to the tent, my lady." Hunter was immediately on his feet.

"It's not necessary," she told him, feeling sad inside that Hunter sounded as if he had his eye on someone back home. She hoped for his sake it was a respectable woman and at least not a whore. Luke really did need a mother. Most likely the types of women Hunter was around all the time weren't going to set a good example for the boy. "Didn't my brother even give you a blanket to use tonight?" she asked, stretching her neck to try to see through the dark.

"I'm hot. I don't need one," he told her. "Sweet dreams, my lady."

"Thank you," she said, entering the tent with Hera and putting the bird on her perch for the night. "Oh, Hera," she whispered. "My heart aches. I think I am falling in love with Hunter and I am the last woman he would probably ever want."

She was awoken later by a clap of thunder and the fluttering of Hera's wings since the noise startled the bird.

"It's all right, girl," she said, getting up to check on and comfort her falcon. The wind picked up causing the flap of her tent to open a little. That is when she heard the sound of rain pelting down against the ground. "Oh, no," she said, peering out of the tent to see Hunter trying to man the fire in the rain. He had no blanket or covering of any kind. Her heart went out to him. Picking up her blanket, she put it over her head. In just her nightshift and with bare feet, she hurried out to join Hunter.

"Fast, get under here," she instructed, holding the blanket open for him.

"My lady, you shouldn't be out in the rain." Hunter ducked and got under the blanket with her. His wet body pressed up against her dry night rail.

"Your clothes are soaking wet," she told him. "You really need to dry off so you don't become ill."

"I'm supposed to be watching the fire," he reminded her. "I promised Robin." They both turned to look at the fire but it had been extinguished in the cold rain and now it only smoked.

"Come into my tent," she told him. "At least until the rain lets up."

"Nay. That wouldn't be proper."

"I insist."

"If I do that and your brother finds out, he'll have my head," said Hunter.

"Then stop talking so loud before you wake him." She put one arm around him and walked with him to her tent. Once inside, she dropped the blanket. Hera made a soft clucking noise from her perch. "It's just Hunter, sweetie," she told her bird while Hunter closed the flap to keep the rain out.

"I'll just stay for a moment," said Hunter, brushing the water off of his arms. "I'm sure the rain will let up soon."

"Yes, I'm sure you are right," she agreed, spreading out the blanket and sitting down upon it. "Sit down next to me, Hunter. But first, you'd better remove your wet clothing."

His head snapped around and even in the dark she could tell that he wondered what she'd meant by that.

"You'll get my bedding wet otherwise," she explained.

"Oh. Yes. All right," he said. She heard him kick off his boots. Then she heard the rustle of clothing and he sat down next to her. She couldn't really see him in the dark. But when she reached out and touched his bare arm she knew that he had removed his wet tunic like she'd told him to do. Just the thought of him sitting there bare-chested made her feel all warm inside.

"I don't think it's right that I'm in here with you," he said in a whisper.

"Shhhh."

"Nay, really, Regina. This isn't right."

"Then just don't tell anyone about it tomorrow."

"Don't worry, I won't. Not if I value keeping my head attached to my body."

She giggled. "You are so sweet, Hunter. Whoever that girl of yours is back home, she is truly lucky to have you."

"What girl?"

"The one you told me about when we were sitting by the fire. Your sweetheart."

"Nay. You've got it all wrong, Regina." She felt him cup her cheek, the heat of his big hand melding with her skin and feeling so inviting. She leaned into his touch and closed her eyes. "You are the sweetheart I was talking about. There is no one else."

"Me?" Her eyes sprang open. "Really? Hunter, are you saying that you want me to be your sweetheart?"

"If things were different, then yes. I would want you not only for my sweetheart but for much more than that."

Regina felt him cup her face in both of his hands next. Then his soft lips caressed hers in a kiss that was so gentle and caring that it was hard to believe such a big and rugged man could be so tender with her.

"What do you mean if things were different?" Her eyes were getting accustomed to the dark now and she could see his face clearly next to hers. They were sitting very close together.

"I am talking about the fact that you are a noble and I am just a commoner," he said.

"Why do you have to bring that up now?" She put her arms around him, feeling his bare chest against her while her hands touched his strong, bare back. Pressing her lips to his chest, she placed kissed trailing across the wide expanse of muscles.

"Mmmm," he moaned, pulling her closer and placing kisses down the back of her neck, managing to send a delicious shiver up her spine. She jerked, but in a good way. "Regina, does that bother you?" he asked in a truly caring voice.

"Not at all. I like your kisses. Very much."

"That's not what I meant." His hands roamed and she didn't stop him. He cupped her breasts and his thumbs flicked over her nipples beneath the fabric causing them to go erect. Her back arched. "I meant the fact that we are from two different worlds, sweetheart."

Mayhap she could have answered if he hadn't slid his hands up the inside of her shift, his fingertips softly making little circles on the skin of her back. Her breathing labored when his hands came up close under her arms and then he palmed her breasts, skin on skin.

"Hunter?"

"Yes?"

"You'd better stop all this talking before someone hears us."

His hands stilled."You're right. I don't want that to happen. Mayhap I should leave."

"It is still raining out there."

"It'll cool me down."

"I'm hot, too. Very, very hot," she said in a breathy whisper, her mouth against his ear. She let her tongue flick out and lick him, making him squirm.

"Regina, don't play with me because I am so hard right now with want for you that I am about ready to burst."

His words excited her even further. She felt a pulsating between her thighs as her body came to life in his embrace. "I want you such as much," she whispered, kissing his chest again wrapping her arms around him. That is when she discovered he wasn't wearing any braies. "You are...totally naked again, aren't you?"

"You make it sound as if I do it a lot."

"Don't you?"

"Only when I'm bathing in the lake." He kissed her behind the ear, causing her to shudder. "Or making love to a beautiful woman."

His hand moved between her thighs next and his fingers brought her to life even more. "Oooh, Hunter. What are you doing to me?" she asked with a tremble to her voice.

"Oh, sweetheart, you really do want this as badly as me. You are wet and ready and I am willing to give you pleasure like you've never felt in your life."

That was all he had to say. She was so excited that she

crawled atop him, straddling her legs around his waist. His arms encompassed her and before she knew what was happening, he had slipped her shift up and over her head, discarding it on the tent floor. Now, she was just as naked as he.

"I want to make sweet love to you, my beautiful Lady-bird," he told her, making Regina's heart about melt.

"Ladybird?" she asked with a giggle.

"What else would I call a lady falconer as talented as you?"

"I like it," she said. "And if you are asking my permission to bed me, I give myself to you wholeheartedly and with no regrets."

He pulled her down to a prone position and her body covered his. She felt the engorgement of his manhood and couldn't help herself from reaching down to touch him. He was so hard yet his soft skin reminded her of silk over steel. As she ran her fingers up and down his length, he moaned softly.

"You don't know what you're doing to me," he whispered in her ear, using his hands to squeeze her back end, pulling her up close to his hardened form. "What do you want me to do?"

"I don't know," she said. "Just do what you usually would in a situation such as this."

Before she knew it, he had rolled her onto her back. He straddled her, holding himself up with his arms so as not to crush her. "You are so beautiful," he said, gently pushing her legs apart with his knee. "I want you for my sweetheart, my sweet, sweet Ladybird."

"I want you as well, my wonderful, handsome Hunter."

He entered her then, surprising her by his length and size as he slid into her womanly warmth. She started to tense, not sure if it would hurt.

"Just relax and let me do all the work," he told her, making her feel safe and secure. "Close your eyes and let yourself go."

They made love gently at first, savoring each touch between them. When she started feeling more comfortable, his thrusts became deeper and faster. Then he took her legs and wrapped them around his hips and she found herself feeling very naughty. But she liked being naughty. Especially with this wonderful man.

"How do you feel?" he asked through a ragged whisper, making her realize he was getting close to release and waiting for her. That thought alone thrilled her. She also found herself excitedby the fact that they were naked and making love in the outdoors.With men sleeping in tents right next to them. Her excitement grew out of control. She wanted this more than anything in her life right now. Her hips moved on their own and she found the rhythm of the dance of love. She had become one with Hunter. Regina griped on to his shoulders, and when she felt herself climbing so high she wanted to scream out, but knew she couldn't. Instead, she raked her nails down his chest, cooing and trying not to scream in ecstasy from what was happening to her right now to make her feel so good.

"Shhh, we need to be quiet," he said, covering her mouth with his as they both found their release together. Regina felt like her falcon flying high and free through the sky, looking down at the ground and all below.

The rain continued to pelt down on the tent, but neither

Regina or Hunter paid any attention to it. Hera squawked from next to them and flapped her wings, making them both giggle softly as they held each other in their arms and tried to regain an even gait of breath.

"That was wonderful," she whispered. "Better than I ever thought it would be."

"So, you've fantasized about making love with me before?" he asked softly.

"Well, actually yes. Ever since that first kiss in your cabin. But that's not what I meant."

"I don't understand."

"Making love," she told him. "It was much more exciting than I ever imagined after hearing about it from my sister and my sister-by-marriage."

He was rubbing circles on her back but his hand suddenly stilled. "Are you saying...this was your first time?"

"Yes."

"First time...ever?"

"Uh huh."

"Damn," she heard him mumble under his breath but she was too fulfilled and happy to even ask why he swore. She cuddled up to him and laid her head on his chest, closing her eyes. Exhausted and spent from a day of hunting and a night of lovemaking, Regina slumbered in Hunter's arms, feeling safe and happy and secure. This was the best night of her entire life!

CHAPTER 11

Regina awoke the next morning feeling happier than she had in a long, long time. She was a full-fledged woman now in every way and didn't regret for a moment having made love with Hunter. He was the only man she had ever really wanted. Now she was his sweetheart and that made her heart soar. His Ladybird, he'd called her. She smiled and rolled over the other way, still dreaming about flying high when she found her release. She had truly felt as free as a bird. Then she heard men's voices outside her tent. Her eyes sprang open thinking she and Hunter were about to be discovered. But when she rolled back over and reached for him, he was no longer there.

"Hunter?" she whispered, sitting up and holding the blanket to her bare chest. The fact that he wasn't there should have relieved her since she was sure it was her brother she'd heard talking outside. Still, it made her feel lonely and empty that he just up and disappeared.

The flap to the tent was open a little and sun streamed

in making a streak across the make-shift bed. Even his clothes and boots were gone. A frightening thought flitted through her mind that this is how she'd feel when Hunter caught and delivered the thief and headed back home. Without her. It wasn't a good feeling at all. She hurriedly got dressed, needing to know what was going on.

Hera became restless on her perch. Almost as restless as Regina felt. Was it from the fact that Hunter wasn't here? Or was it because he had been here in the first place? Confusion muddled her mind.

"Come on, Hera. Let's go find Hunter." She put on her glove and picked up her bird and stepped outside the tent.

Hunter tried his hardest to get the fire going again this morning, but it was too late. Robin had just emerged from his own tent, followed by his squire and the other men. If Hunter hadn't been sleeping with Regina, mayhap he would have realized that the rain had stopped hours ago and morning was here. Thankfully, he had at least got out of Regina's tent before anyone discovered just what happened between them last night.

"What happened to the fire, Hunter?" asked Robin. "I'm chilled from the rain last night and would like to warm up before we head for home."

"I'm sorry, my lord. The rain was too much for it and the wood is too wet to light. I'm afraid I didn't do my job as well as I should have."

"I'd beg to differ about that." Regina walked out of the tent with Hera on her arm.

Hunter felt like all hell was about to break loose. Was

she perhaps talking about what happened last night between them? Was it her way of saying a job well done? God's eyes, what had he been thinking? Bedding a noblewoman could land him in the dungeon. Or on the gallows. Taking a noblewoman's virginity had to be even a worse offense somehow, he was sure. Now, because he'd been so enamored by her and he'd had a weak moment, the girl was ruined for life. She'd never be able to be betrothed to any nobleman or marry for an alliance in the future. His lovemaking had seen to that. If only he'd never have gone into the tent with her, none of this would be happening right now.

Once again, his sister's judging voice swarmed his head. *What did you do? What were you thinking? You just used the girl for your own needs, never thinking of her and her needs. Her future.*

God's eyes, he thought to himself. What the hell had he done?

"Regina, what are you talking about?" asked Robin.

"Brother, you left Hunter out here by himself last night in the rain without even giving him a blanket or any kind of cover. That was very insensitive of you."

"Nay, it wasn't. I don't mind." Hunter didn't want this conversation to get back to last night and tried his hardest to push it in any other direction.

"Baldwin, take apart my sister's tent," ordered Robin. "Since we have no fire, we'll be on our way as soon as the tents are packed."

"Yes, my lord," said his squire, going inside Regina's tent.

"For being out in the rain all night, you're not as wet as I would have expected you to be," said Robin looking at Hunter's clothes.

"Nay, my lord. I was able to...find shelter." Hunter wasn't lying, even if he didn't say where that shelter might have been.

"Well, I'm glad to hear that," said Robin with a yawn. "So how was your first hunt? Was it everything you expected?"

He looked over and his eyes locked with Regina's. Damn, just looking at her made him go weak in the knees. "It was more than I expected, my lord. With a few surprises thrown in," he answered. Regina smiled.

"Surprises? What kind of surprises?" asked Robin, but before anyone could answer, his squire ran out of the tent holding on to Regina's blanket.

"My lady, are you hurt?"

"Nay, why do you ask?" she answered.

"There is blood on your blanket. I thought mayhap you'd cut yourself." He held up the blanket, displaying the proof of Regina's loss of virginity to every man there. Hunter groaned to himself and closed his eyes. His life was about to end right here, right now.

"Regina? What is that?" asked Robin.

"It...it's my flux" she said softly, looking at the ground.

"Oh, I see," said Robin clearing his throat. "Well, at least you're not hurt."

Hunter's eyes popped open. He couldn't believe what just happened. Such a stroke of luck because of Regina's quick thinking. She may have just saved his ass from landing in the dungeon.

"Nay, I'm not hurt," she said, once again looking at Hunter. What the hell did she want him to say?

"Yes. Yes, it is good you are not hurt," he choked out. Hunter bent over to fix his boot, his tunic falling open as he did so.

"Hunter? Are those scratch marks on your chest?" Robin walked over to inspect them. Hunter's heart stilled. He'd almost forgotten that Regina had raked her nails down his chest in the throw of their vivid lovemaking. Now, he knew he was about to die for sure.

"It was my fault," Regina called out, making Robin stop in his tracks and slowly turn.

God's teeth, was she really going to tell him? What the hell was the matter with her?

"Your fault, Sister? How so?" Robin slowly walked back to her. Regina's chin rose in the air as she held her bird high atop her arm. She didn't look at all frightened. Shouldn't she be running for her horse by now? Hunter knew that is what he felt he should be doing.

"I was careless and put Hera too close to Hunter at the campfire last night after the rest of you had retired. He moved to stoke the fire and Hera was frightened, and scratched him. Those marks on Hunter's chest are from the bird."

"Is that right, Hunter?" Robin looked back at him. The only way to get out of this without being sentenced was to go along with the lie. Lies again. Damn it, he hated having to live this way.

"Honestly, I don't even remember the bird scratching me," he said, getting an odd look from Robin. "I think I was too tired to think straight after such a big day."

"Is that right?" Robin's gaze flashed from Hunter to Regina and back to Hunter again.

"He was tired, that's true," said Regina. "So tired that he went to bed right after the rest of you."

"To sleep," Hunter interjected. "I didn't have a bed of course. I mean, my bed was here. By the fire."

"Didn't you wake up when it started raining on you?" Robin had to know something was going on.

"I found shelter. Like I told you," said Hunter. "I'm sorry once again for letting the fire go out."

"Well, it's over now," said Robin. "I suppose no harm has been done, so what does it matter?"

"Aye," agreed Hunter, his gaze going back to Regina. He couldn't stop feeling like harm was done. Harm that could not be undone. Bid the devil, he'd just ruined a lady and couldn't do a damn thing about it.

The ride home was long and uncomfortable. Hunter did his best to ignore Regina, not wanting to talk about last night and not wanting Robin watching them like a hawk anymore either. He needed to think this over. By himself. He hated ignoring the girl, but right now he felt as if this was what he had to do to protect both of them from being exposed. Damn, life never seemed to get any easier.

Hunter, you are such a fool, came his departed sister's voice in his head once again. *What made you think you had the right to even touch a noblewoman let alone take her virginity? You ruined her now for life. Because of you, she has no chance to ever be happy.*

Damn it, his dead sister kept taunting him and it was not only about his mistakes with Luke, but about his personal life now. His love life to be exact. He just couldn't stand it anymore. He wanted his sister's chastising out of his head forever.

"Get away from me," he warned his sister's ghost, but Regina had rode up next to him at that same moment and thought he was talking to her.

"Get away from you? What did I do to make you so angry, Hunter? Why are you talking to me that way?" She rode with Hera on her glove, looking regal and elegant as always. The spring air smelled fresh and crisp and it seemed everything was budding to life all around them.

"Nay, Regina. I wasn't talking to you."

She scowled. "Well, I hardly think you were talking to Hera."

"Nay. Nay, I wasn't talking to her either."

"What is the matter with you, Hunter?" she asked, sounding more than perturbed with him. "You have been ignoring me all morning."

"Regina, I think it might be better if we make distance between us for a while."

"What? Why?" she asked, first sounding sad and then sounding angry. "Are you ashamed of what we did together?"

"Shhh," he said, looking around, hoping none of the men had heard her.

"Hunter, I'm not going to hide in the shadows anymore. It is my life and I can do what I please."

"Yes, you can, but I can't."

"What does that mean?"

"Regina, can we talk about this later?"

"How, when you want us to make distance between us?"

"I mean, can we discuss it at a better time?"

"Better time? No, Hunter we can't. This time is as good as any. We have feelings for each other and I don't see why we have to hide them."

"I'm no good for you, sweetheart. You should find a nobleman who will make you happy." It's not what Hunter really wanted, but he didn't want her saddled with a man like him for the rest of her life either.

"I don't want a nobleman," she spat. "If I did, I would have found one long before now. And I don't want you telling me what I should or shouldn't do, either." She sped off on her horse in a huff, making Hunter feel even worse than before. Part of him wanted to ride after Regina and stop her and tell her that he loved her and wanted to be with her. Forever. But another part of him kept telling him that he had done a bad thing and that he didn't deserve her. After all, Regina was goodness and light, poise and grace. The woman was smart and sassy and more than strong in every aspect of her life. She had a keen skill with training birds like no man could ever attain, he was sure. She had so much to offer.

He had so little.

Damn, he was confused right now and only hoped that once they got back to the castle he could sort out his thoughts in his head and know the right thing to do. Know how to fix his mistake and make everything better.

Well, it didn't take long to figure out that he was wrong.

When they rode through the gates of Shrewsbury Castle, Roger the falconer ran out from the mews to meet them. He had a look of terror on his face. Hunter knew that whatever the boy had to say, it wasn't going to be good and neither would it make Regina happy.

"Roger, how are you feeling?" asked Regina from atop

her horse, obviously not noticing that the boy was in turmoil. She dismounted, not needing the help of a man, managing to keep Hera on her glove.

"My lady, I am so sorry," cried Roger. "I honestly don't know how it even happened."

"What on earth are you talking about?" Regina dug a piece of raw meat from her bag and fed it to the bird.

"When I returned to the mews this morning is when I noticed. I thought mayhap you had taken both birds on the hunting trip, but Cassian said that you hadn't.

"Roger?" asked Regina with worry in her voice now. "What are you trying to say?"

"It's horrible, my lady. Just awful. The thief has struck again, and this time he has stolen from the mews. Lady Regina, I am sorry to tell you that Lightning is gone!"

CHAPTER 12

"Nay, this can't be happening!" Regina hurried into the mews with Hunter and the rest of the men following right at her heels.

"Where's Cassian?" shouted Robin. "Get him out here, now!"

"I'm here, my lord," said Cassian walking out of a shadow.

"Where were you when this happened?" asked Robin.

"It happened last night, I believe. While I was sleeping," said the old man.

"Did you hear anyone in the mews last night?" asked Hunter.

"Nay." The man shook his head.

"No, of course not," mumbled Hunter, since the man was nearly deaf and probably slept through the storm as well.

Regina put Hera on her perch and then proceeded to check on Dewdrop and Cloud.

"Are the other birds all right?" Hunter asked, coming up behind her.

"They're fine," she answered. "But Lightning is gone! Oh, Hunter, please find her. I am so upset that my whole body is shaking. I pray she is all right."

"Damn it! I should have been here doing my job instead of being out on the hunt," spat Hunter. "I blame myself that this happened."

"What do you mean?" asked one of the huntsmen. "How is it your fault, my lord?"

"Yes, and what do you mean your job?" asked Robin's squire. "I don't understand."

Al and Sage entered the mews next, followed by Fred. Luke was following slowly but walking as if he'd never been injured at all. He carried Inky in his arms.

"What's going on out here?" asked Sage. "I heard the commotion and yelling all the way from the keep."

"Oh, Sage, it's awful," cried Regina, running to the woman. "The thief has struck again and this time he took Lightning."

"I will put a stop to this," Hunter spoke up. "I swear I will find this thief and he will hang for what he's done."

"Do you really think you can find him?" asked Baldwin.

"I can. It's my job and what I do."

"Why does he keep saying that?" asked Paul.

"Lord Robin, you may as well tell them all. There is no sense keeping my identity a secret any longer," said Hunter.

"You're right," agreed Robin. "Everyone, Hunter Chase is a thief-taker who I hired to find and bring in the thief who has been robbing us."

"Ah ha! That's how I know you," said Al. "I thought you

seemed familiar. You're that thief-taker who lives in the woods outside of town, aren't you?"

"I am," Hunter admitted.

"He's naught but a damned mercenary, selling his sword to the highest bidder," said Cassian with a sneer. "Just like his old man."

"What?" Regina blinked several times, looking over at Hunter. "What is he talking about, Hunter?"

"It's true, Lady Regina," said Hunter, swallowing his pride. "I was a mercenary for many years. I started when I was only thirteen."

"So you...killed people when you were only Luke's age?" Regina was standing near him but took a step backward when she said it. It felt horrible. She acted as if she were appalled or frightened of him now. That is the last thing he ever wanted. They had been intimate and it felt good. It was magical and special. Now, he was sure Regina would never even want to speak to him again and he couldn't say he blamed her.

"I'm not proud of my past," said Hunter in a humble manner. "Believe me, it wasn't my choice. I wish my life had been different. I was a child who was reared in a dishonorable manner, and I hate it. But it is in the past now, Lady Regina. There is nothing I can do to change it." He wanted her to understand that he was no longer the man he used to be. "I don't kill anymore unless it is in self-defense. I rarely even use my weapons to bring in thieves. I swear it is the truth. I am doing all I can to change the darkness of my past."

"Really." Regina seemed to look down her nose at him now. "I find that hard to believe since you've given your thirteen-year-old nephew a deadly sword. Your words belie your actions."

"My uncle always says to look at people's actions to know what is really going on," Luke spoke up, not making things any easier.

"Now wait a minute. That was different," Hunter said in his defense. "The sword I gave Luke was once my father's and the only thing I have left to remember him by. I wanted to pass it down."

"Odd how you hold so precious a weapon that has been used to kill on command, yet you want me to believe you reject your past." Regina was making him feel even worse. "I'm sorry, Hunter Chase, but I just can't believe you about anything anymore."

There was a lull in the conversation. Hunter felt Regina's accusations as naught but a knife twisting in his heart. Mayhap she was right. Mayhap he wasn't any different than his father before him.

You should have told Lady Regina about your past, Hunter, came that damned nagging voice of his late sister in his head once again. *She'll never want you now. Why would she? You are no better than an assassin and she is a lady. You are raising Luke the way your father raised you and you should be ashamed. What were you thinking, you fool?*

"Excuse me, everyone," said Hunter, feeling as if he wanted to retch. Last night was one of the best times of his life but today was one of the worst. He couldn't live like this anymore. Hunter pushed his way through the crowd and made his way out the door. "I have a thief to catch, and by God the damned man better be worried. Because when I get my hands on him, he is going to be more than sorry."

. . .

Regina stood watching as Hunter left the mews, not sure what to think anymore. She felt numb. Lightning was gone and the man she thought she loved was proving to be naught but a liar. She'd given him her virginity! She gave him her heart. She thought she was safe in his arms but now she just found out he was naught but a man who killed on command for money. Her life was falling apart around her and this time she wasn't sure she'd be able to pick up the pieces and put it back together.

"Everyone, get back to work," commanded Robin, clearing out the mews except for Roger and Cassian. "Sister, are you all right?" Robin put his hand on Regina's shoulder.

"Nay, I'm not all right," she spat. "How in heaven's name could I be? One of my babies has been abducted and I'm not going to be happy until you find the thief and execute him. Roger, please don't leave the birds alone for one moment," she commanded. Not wanting to cry in front of the men, Regina turned and ran from the mews.

She didn't stop running until she entered her chamber and slammed the door closed behind her. Wanting to be alone and think, she threw herself down on the bed and cried. A few minutes later she heard a soft knocking at her door. Thinking it was Hunter, she decided she didn't want to talk to him. Nay, she wanted nothing to do with him at all.

"Go away! Leave me alone!" she shouted, saying the same words back to him that he'd said to her on their ride home even though she hadn't understood why he'd been acting that way.

The door squeaked open and Sage stuck her head into the room. "Regina? Can I come in, please?"

"Oh, it's you, Sage." Regina sat up and used a hand cloth to wipe away her tears. "Yes, come in. I welcome your presence. Just not...his."

"I am so sorry about Lightning being stolen." Sage sat down to comfort her, putting her arm around her shoulder. "Don't even think a bad thought. I am sure Hunter will find the thief as well as the bird. He is good as what he does."

"Hmmph," she snorted. "Mayhap a little too good because he sure had me fooled."

"What do you mean?" asked Sage.

"Nothing. Nothing at all."

"I have a feeling you are not talking about Hunter's profession of being a thief-taker, are you?"

"Nay, I'm not."

"Oh. You are upset about the fact he was a mercenary at one time, aren't you?"

"Well, yes. Mercenaries are horrible men with no morals, conscience or even souls. They will kill anyone if the pay is good enough. This is very upsetting to me, Sage. I thought Hunter was different. I mean, did you and Robin know he'd been a mercenary?"

"Nay, we didn't. Your father hired Hunter and knew Hunter's father, Robert. I'm sure Madoc must have known. But you heard Hunter. It was the way he was brought up, he couldn't help it. No one can change the past."

"Nay, I suppose not. And neither can I change my past with him either." Thoughts of their lovemaking filled her head as well as Hunter ignoring her afterwards. She also couldn't accept who he really was and how he'd kept it from her. It was all too much for her to handle, given the fact she'd just lost her peregrine falcon that was like a child to her. She couldn't stop herself from bawling.

"He lied to me, Sage."

"He didn't lie. Unless you asked him directly if he'd been a mercenary and he denied it."

"Nay. Of course not. How would I have known?"

"Regina, everything will be all right," said Sage, not knowing half of her problems. "Just have faith. Trust Hunter."

"Trust him? Hah! That is what got me in this situation in the first place. I never should have trusted him and let him into my life. Nay, I made a big mistake. I never should have let him touch me."

"Touch you?" Sage reached up and gently smoothed back Regina's hair. "Is there something else you'd like to tell me? Were you and Hunter...intimately involved?"

Regina felt as if she would die if she didn't confide in someone soon. Since her sisters weren't here to talk to, and she'd never mention this in a million years to Robin, she felt Sage was her only and best choice. Sage had become a good friend to Regina since she'd married Robin.

"Yes, Sage, he did touch me," she admitted with a sniffle. She blotted her eyes and then continued. "Hunter and I...we made love last night."

"Oh!" Sage's eyes opened wide and she held a hand to her heart. "I see. Does Robin know about this?"

"Nay! And neither will you ever tell him."

"Honey, did Hunter force himself on you? Because if he did, you need to let your brother know at once."

That only made Regina cry even more. "Hunter didn't

force himself on me. If anything, I was the one who initiated it."

"Then you have feelings for the man?"

"No! Yes. Oh, I don't know. I am so confused. I thought I was falling in love with him, Sage. But now I'm not sure what to think."

"Does he feel the same way about you?"

"I thought he did." She blew her nose in the cloth. "He even called me his Ladybird when I was in his arms."

"Ladybird?" Sage smiled. "Oh, that is cute. I like it."

"So do I." Regina wrung the cloth in her hands.

"Then what's the problem, Regina?"

"I...he...oh, I don't know. Last night was wonderful. Better than I had ever imagined it could be. I'm sure he thought so too. Then, it just seemed like he was ignoring me all morning and I don't know why. It was like he regretted what we did together."

"You need to talk to him, Regina."

"I can't. Nay. I don't want to."

"It is unfair of you to judge the man simply by what you think he might or might not be feeling. After all, he's had a hard life. He had been raised at a young age as a mercenary and then lost everyone he ever loved. He's been left with an unruly boy to raise all by himself. And as you have noticed it doesn't seem to be going well. Did you ever consider that mayhap he is trying to do his best but it is just not good enough for anyone?"

"Oh, Sage, do you really think that is how he feels?" Regina started wondering if mayhap she'd judged Hunter too harshly, just like Sage said.

"I am only telling you this from experience. I was once a

person with nothing, trying to raise my siblings on my own. I know how hard it can be. You are a noble, Regina. Your life has been good and easy. You've always had everything you ever needed or could possibly want."

"Nay, not everything," she said sadly.

"What do you mean?"

"I thought I was happy just raising my birds, Sage. But once I met Hunter, I started to realize how empty my life really was without having someone—having a man to love. A man like Hunter."

"Mayhap he is that man you've always wanted and you just didn't know it until now. If you think at all this might be true, I urge you to go and talk to him right away. Talk about your relationship with him and tell him how you feel. Be sure to ask him how he is feeling as well. Do it before he finds the thief and leaves the castle. Do it before the best thing that ever happened to you goes out that door forever."

CHAPTER 13

Frustrated as all hell, Hunter made his way back to his chamber to try to calm down before he continued his search for the thief. He entered his room, stomping over and sitting down on a chair with his head between his hands.

"What the hell is happening to me?" he mumbled, not expecting an answer. Then, that damned voice in his head started up again, about driving him mad.

You failed, Hunter. You lost Luke's love and now you've lost Regina's, too. You don't deserve it. You have no right raising a child. You shouldn't be in the castle either. Find your thief and go back to your pathetic hut in the woods. You were better off as a bloody mercenary. All you know is how to fight and how to kill. You know nothing of love and never will.

"Nay, damn it. Stop it!" he screamed, jumping up so abruptly that the chair fell over behind him. Part of him believed the voice of his late sister and it didn't feel good at all. Mayhap he didn't deserve to be here dressed like a noble and sleeping in a bed that could fit four. Perhaps he should just leave and go back to his horrible life in the woods. Alone.

"Nay, I won't leave before I find the thief. I gave my word and I will keep it. I will do the job I was hired to do." He looked down at his clothes. The clothes of a noble. "But not dressed like this, I won't."

It wasn't who he was and he was tired of lying. If he was going to earn the respect of anyone, especially Regina, he would do it as himself. Not as someone else.

He opened a trunk in the room, rummaging around for his clothes. The clothes he'd been wearing when he first arrived here at Shrewsbury Castle. He'd put them in here somewhere and wanted to take them back.

Flipping open the lid on the trunk, he found his tunic and breeches right on top and donned them quickly. Then he kicked off the boots the nobles had given him, going back to the trunk to try to find his.

He dug to the bottom, and pulled out what he thought was his boots. That's when he realized these weren't his at all. These were the boots that Luke had been wearing when he tripped. It irked him because he hadn't had time to even reprimand the boy about it yet.

Throwing them down, he dug deeper. That's when he found a crossbow wrapped up in Luke's tunic.

"What the hell?" Hunter ran his hand over the crossbow in thought. He was sure this wasn't in here when they'd first arrived. Suddenly, he saw things clear as day. Hadn't Luke asked for not only a black cat but also a pair of boots and a crossbow? It was a little too convenient that Hunter would find most of these things in here.

Placing the crossbow on the floor, he dug through the trunk some more.

"Ouch!" he spat, pricking his finger on something sharp. He picked it up and his mouth fell open. It was a lady's brooch. That is, a brooch in the shape of a hawk with diamonds on the tips of the wings and a ruby for its eye. "God's teeth, this can't be true."

Hunter felt like a fool. He'd been so infatuated with Regina that he hadn't even seen what was right under his own nose. "Luke is a thief," he muttered, his heart breaking, but the proof was as clear as day. Hadn't the boy been acting strange lately? And things he'd always wanted kept appearing in his life like magic. "Damn it, Luke. Why? Why!"

There came a knock on his door and he spun around. "Who is it?" he ground out.

"Hunter?" came a muffled voice from the other side. "It's me. Regina. Can we talk?"

"Hell, not now," he grumbled. This was the worst possible timing of all. He needed to talk to Luke, not Regina. Then again, if he turned her away, things might be over between them forever. Not that they already weren't. "Just a minute," he said, tossing the brooch back in the trunk and then the boots and crossbow and slamming the lid shut.

He hurried to the door and opened it to see his beautiful angel standing there. All he wanted to do was to pull her into his embrace and hug and kiss her and tell her that he never wanted to leave her side.

But he wouldn't. He couldn't. Things were not the same between them anymore.

"Can I come in?" she asked. He saw her red nose and wet eyes and knew she'd been crying.

"I don't know. I don't think it's a good idea, Regina." He didn't move aside to let her enter. If he were alone with her again, he'd only want to comfort her and hold her and kiss her. He already knew how well that would turn out. Nay, he couldn't be alone with her again. "Perhaps we can talk while we walk." He started back across the room, looking for his damned boots.

"Hunter, I'm scared. I just heard from Robin that while we were gone the thief also stole one of the huntsmen's crossbows."

He stopped in his tracks. "God's eyes, nay," he said, running a hand through his hair. He looked back over his shoulder at the trunk. So, it seemed his suspicions were correct. He had raised a thief and now had to decide whether to turn in the boy or not.

"Can we please talk right here inside your room?" she begged him. "There is something I want to say to you but I want to do it in private."

"Regina, I don't think—"

Too late. She entered the room anyway. With a sigh, he walked over and closed the door.

"Hunter, I will make this fast," she told him.

"Good. Because I have a lot to do."

She paced the room and wrung her hands as she spoke. "First of all, I am not happy at all that you didn't tell me about your past. Being a mercenary, I mean."

"I try to forget about that time in my life," he told her. "Besides, what does it matter? It has no effect on the job I was hired to do here at Shrewsbury Castle."

"What does it matter?" she repeated his words, shaking her head as she spoke. "It matters to me," she told him, stopping and looking up with concern in her eyes.

"Regina, what can I say? I'm sorry. Sorry for not telling you and sorry that it is part of my dark past at all."

"Dark past? Hunter, is there more you're not telling me?"

"Nothing more other than the fact I was unwanted and unloved and could never be the person everyone else seemed to want me to be."

"Oh, Hunter, I'm so sorry," she said, dropping her hands to her side.

"Huh?" he asked in confusion, knowing he should be the one apologizing to her but now she was apologizing to him. None of this made sense.

"I accept you for who you are." She smiled and walked over and took his hands in hers.

"Regina, please," he said in a soft voice. "You don't have to do this."

"I cherish the time we spent together," she continued. "I don't regret making love with you, and I want you to know that I don't care any longer about your past."

"You—don't?" He shook his head. "I thought you just said you were upset that I was a mercenary. That I pretended to be someone I wasn't."

"I know. I can't even think straight because I am so worried about Lightning. Besides, I think I was just more upset by the fact that you didn't tell me about it."

"Regina, now you're the one lying." He looked down at her in a knowing manner.

"All right, I guess I am. Yes, it disturbs me horribly, but Sage helped me to realize that it wasn't your fault. You were just a child and doing what you were told to do. I will come to terms with that, but please be patient with me. I am trying my hardest."

"Wait a minute. Did you talk to Sage about me?"

"Yes. I needed another woman's thoughts."

"I see," he said, realizing he was no different, having talked to William about her. "What about the fact I gave my father's sword to Luke and took him along on my jobs? Doesn't that bother you?"

She hesitated for a moment, then bit her lip and shook her head. "You were trying to save the memory of the only parent who cared for you. I understand that."

"Yes, That's right, I was."

"And you are doing the best you can raising the boy. I know it isn't easy."

"I am," he said, wondering why she was being so understanding all of a sudden. It almost made him feel guiltier than he did before.

"At least Luke doesn't carry the sword around with him." She seemed more settled with that thought.

"Nay, he doesn't. Or at least not lately," said Hunter, looking around the room wondering where the boy put the sword and hoping he hadn't decided to flash it around to his friends again. He had told Luke to leave it in the room and by God he hoped the boy actually listened.

"Hunter, I was upset with you because you were ignoring me this morning. That is what started this all. After the wonderful night we spent together, I didn't understand why you would treat me that way. It made me feel like you regretted what we did."

"Nay, that's not true." He took her by the hands. "I don't regret making love to you, Regina. I could never regret spending one minute with you. You are the kindest, smartest, most beautiful woman I've ever met. I guess I just can't understand why you would want someone like me at all."

"Is that why you were ignoring me?" She looked up to him with her big hazel eyes, waiting for his honest answer.

"Partially," he said softly.

"Oh, Hunter, I think I am falling in love with you and I need to know how you feel about me."

"Regina, you have no idea how much I care for you." He pulled her into his arms, kissing her atop the head. "I only tried to distance myself from you because I realized that I ruined you."

"Ruined me? How so?"

"I took your virginity. That is something you can never get back."

She pulled away and looked up at him. "You didn't take anything that I wasn't willing to give."

"I don't deserve you, and you know it. I am not good for you, Regina."

"If anything, you should think I am not good enough for you. I acted like a whore, making love with a man to whom I wasn't married."

"Nay, never say that," he told her, kissing her gently on her lips. "You are a noble, an honorable lady and you always will be. I only regret that now your reputation is soiled. Because of me, you will never be able to marry a nobleman. All because of one night of passion. Of what we did together."

"If I had wanted to marry a nobleman, don't you think I would have done so by now?" she asked him.

"I don't know. Why haven't you been betrothed by now? You are certainly of marrying age."

"It's because I never thought I needed or wanted a man. Not until I met you." She reached up and touched him on the cheek. Her soft skin against his felt so inviting that he moaned softly and closed his eyes. "Hunter, I love you."

His eyes shot open. "You don't really meant that. You couldn't love a man like me."

"Are you calling me a liar?"

"Nay. I'm the liar. But I'm done with lying, sweetheart." He pulled her into his arms and kissed her with undeniable passion. "I do love you, my Ladybird. I swear, if I wasn't just a commoner, I'd be asking you to marry me right now."

"Well, why don't you?" She looked at him and bit at her lip.

"What do you mean?" His heart stilled.

"Hunter, I am sure you are not a stranger to the fact that most of the Blake siblings have been marrying commoners lately."

"Yes, I have heard. So?"

"So, if we wanted to get married, it would be no different."

"Your father wouldn't object?"

"I don't see why. He knew your father. They were friends. He was the one to bring us together if you look at it from a different angle."

"I suppose. I see your point."

"Do you love me?"

"Yes. Yes, I think I do."

"And I love you."

"So, you believe we should be together?"

She nodded. "Don't you?"

"What I think and what I want are two different things entirely."

You can't have her. Don't even think she really loves you because she doesn't.

"Nay. I won't listen to you anymore!" he shouted.

She released him and stepped back, almost in fear. "What?" she gasped.

"Oh, sweetheart, nay. I am not talking to you." He reached out for her again.

"Well, I don't see anyone else in here." She looked around the room..

"Nay, it's my sister."

"I thought you said your sister was dead."

"She is. But I've been hearing Mary's condescending voice in my head for years now, telling me I can't do anything right and that I am no good."

"That's not true, Hunter."

"I could never seem to please my older sister. I think she hated me, mainly because I was a bastard from another father."

"Oh, I am so sorry, Hunter. I had no idea that you were hearing demons in your head." She stroked his cheek gently. "You need to push those nasty voices away. They are only going to ruin your life as well as drive you crazy."

"I know you're right. But it isn't easy."

"Then, let me help you try." She kissed him deeply and ran her hands through his hair.

Hunter could see where this was going. "Regina, I can't take you to bed again."

"What?" She looked so disappointed.

"Not before I ask you something very important."

"What is it, Hunter?"

He got down in front of her on one knee, taking her hands in his. "I know I don't have much to offer, sweetheart, and I feel crazy for even considering this. I can give you my protection and my love, if that is enough for you."

"Hunter? Why are you kneeling?"

"I think I'm in love with you, Ladybird. I would like nothing more than if you would marry me and be my wife."

"I can't believe this is happening." Regina knelt down and looked him in the eye. "Hunter, I don't want you to ever feel like you are not as good as anyone else. You are a good man, so don't forget that. Any woman would be lucky to be your wife."

"But?" He held his breath while he waited for her answer. That nasty voice in his head started to return to put doubt in the fact he was doing the right thing. Then he pushed the voice out of his mind, focusing on the wonderful woman before him, drinking in the love that was emanating from her.

"No buts. Yes, I would be honored to be your wife, Hunter Chase. I know we will always be happy together."

"Oh, Regina." He pulled her into a hug, his heart opening like it never had before. He'd found a woman who accepted him, forgave him and loved him all at the same time. It was a dream for a man like him and he honestly wasn't sure he was really awake. "I promise to be the best husband I can be."

"I promise to be the best wife I can be. Now, kiss me, Hunter. This is way too much talking."

He did kiss her. Then he picked her up in his arms and

carried her to the bed, placing her down softly upon the lush mattress. They both knew what they wanted and no one would ever stop them because they wouldn't let that happen. They made love atop the bed, sharing their passion and love for each other and this time not holding back their cries of release. For a short wonderful while all their troubles had disappeared.

"Regina, I would love to stay right here in bed with you for a week, but I have a thief to catch right now." He kissed her on the nose and then got up and started to dress.

"Yes, and a falcon to find, don't forget." Regina got up and dressed as well. "Hunter, I am so scared that I'll never see Lightning again."

"Don't be. I promise you that I will find her and she will be just fine. Let me find my boots and I'll get my head back into my work."

"Mayhap they're in here," she said, walking over and flipping open the trunk.

"Regina, no!" It was too late to stop her.

"What's this?" She picked up the crossbow.When she did, the hawk brooch fell to the floor at her feet. "It's Sage's brooch." She put down the crossbow and picked up the pin. "Hunter, I don't understand. What are these things doing here?"

"I don't really know, and that's the truth," he told her, finding his boots and putting them on. "I have just discovered them a few minutes ago, not unlike you. Regina, I have an awful suspicion that Luke might be the thief."

CHAPTER 14

"Luke, come out here right now. I need to talk to you." Hunter stood in the door of the stables, calling out his young nephew.

Regina was with him, fingering the brooch, feeling it in her heart that the boy couldn't possibly be the thief they hunted.

"What is it, Hunter?" Luke walked out with the cat in his arms and Fred right behind him.

"Alone," said Hunter in a commanding voice. "Give the cat to Fred and follow me."

"But we were just going to—"

"Now!" shouted Hunter, taking the cat from him and pushing her into Fred's arms. Then he grabbed Luke by the back of the tunic and yanked him toward him.

"Hunter, mayhap you don't need to be so rough," suggested Regina, seeing this was already not going well.

"You're hurting me," cried Luke, even though Regina could see that the boy was only acting.

"We can talk in the mews," said Regina. "I'll ask Cassian and Roger to step out. That will give us some privacy."

"Good idea," said Hunter, following her with the boy still in his grip.

"Lady Regina. Lord Hunter," said Roger when they walked into the mews. "Did you find Lightning yet?"

"It's just Hunter without the Lord," Hunter corrected him."And no, we haven't found the missing bird yet."

"Roger, can you and Cassian please step out for a minute? We'd like a little privacy," Regina told him.

"Of course. Cassian. Cassian!" Roger yelled to the older man who slowly turned around. "Let's go," said Roger, waving his arm. Cassian eyed them up curiously, but followed Roger out of the mews.

"Let go of me." Luke struggled against Hunter's hold.

"We need to talk," said Hunter.

"About what?"

"I found a crossbow in the trunk in our chamber. I also found this." Hunter held out his hand and Regina gave him the brooch. He held it up and Luke's disposition suddenly changed. The boy looked to the ground and kicked at the straw rushes on the floor. "Did you steal these things, Luke?" asked Hunter. "I want the truth, so don't even think of lying."

"Nay. I didn't steal them." Luke couldn't look at Hunter and Regina realized the boy was not telling the truth. Or at least not the whole truth.

"I don't believe you," snapped Hunter.

"Hunter, please." Regina took back the brooch from him. "This brooch was missing before you and Luke ever came to the castle. He couldn't have stolen it."

"True, but why has it suddenly appeared in a trunk in our chamber?" asked Hunter.

"I was just holding it for someone," explained Luke.

"Holding it? Holding a stolen item? Who the hell for?" Hunter demanded to know.

Luke looked down and kicked at the floor again. "I don't want to tell you."

"Then why don't you start by telling me where you got the crossbow, the boots and while you're at it, the cat, too. After all, it is odd that you told me you wanted those things and as soon as we got here you suddenly had them." Hunter was not happy with the boy and Regina couldn't blame him. Still, she could see he was scaring the boy and that Luke would only end up rebelling if Hunter didn't pull back.

"Let me try," she said softly, resting her hand on Hunter's arm.

"Be my guest." Hunter turned away and crossed his arms.

"Luke, sit down," said Regina, sitting on a wooden bench and patting the seat next to her.

"I don't want to sit." Anything they suggested now, the boy was sure to object.

Hunter looked up as if he were going to command the boy to sit, but Regina raised her hand in the air to stop him. "That's fine," she said, playing with the brooch. "I'm really sad about Lightning being stolen. I am scared that I might never see her again."

"I didn't take her. Honest, I didn't." Luke's eyes opened wide.

"I know you didn't," said Regina. "I just want you to

know that it isn't right for anyone to steal anything. No matter how small or insignificant it might be."

"I didn't steal nothing, Lady Regina. I got the boots by bluffing," Luke told her. "Hunter does it all the time."

She saw Hunter look up and then drop his arms to his sides, shaking his head slowly.

"Hunter?" Regina gave him an opportunity to explain what this meant.

"Luke, I was wrong by bluffing to get things I wanted," said Hunter. "You shouldn't do it either. It's just not right."

"Bluffing? What exactly does that mean?" She looked over to Hunter once again.

"Lying," said Hunter softly.

"Oh." She sighed and put the brooch into a pouch at her side.

"I won the boots playing cards with the guards," Luke continued. "Hunter taught me how to gamble."

"He did, did he?" She didn't need to even look at Hunter to know he was probably cringing right now.

"Even though I bluffed and didn't really have a winning hand, I still won the game." Luke slowly sat down next to Regina. "You believe me, Lady Regina, don't you?"

Regina's gaze shot over to Hunter and then back to the boy. "Yes. Yes, we both believe you. Right, Hunter?"

She was afraid Hunter was going to object, but when she shook her head slowly, he went along with her plan.

"Yes, I believe you, Luke." Hunter came over and sat on the bench next to Luke, making it cozy between the three of them. "What about the cat? William from town says Inky has a white spot on her paw just like his did. He swears she is his cat."

"She is," said Luke, looking so sad. "It was Fred's idea."

"What do you mean?" asked Regina, really having hoped that this part wasn't true. She saw how happy the cat had made the boy and how much love he gave her.

"Well, I told Fred I always wanted a black cat," Luke explained. "Fred said he saw one in William's tailor shop and said I should take her."

"So you really were hanging out in front of the tailor's like William said?" asked Hunter.

"Even though Fred wanted me to take her, I just wanted to pet her," protested Luke. "Then it was Fred's idea to start feeding her. Once we did, she started to follow us."

"All the way back to the castle, I'll bet," said Hunter. "With a little coaxing?"

"Yes. I'm sorry," said Luke. "But I really love Inky. Do I have to give her back?"

Hunter looked over to Regina, obviously not sure what to say.

"I'm sure if we talk to William he might let us buy her from him," suggested Regina.

"Really?" Luke came to life, becoming excited by the idea.

"Slow down," said Hunter. "We will discuss the cat later. Right now, you need to tell me more. Like how in heaven's name did you get a crossbow? I'm sure you didn't win that in a game of chance."

"Nay, I traded for it." Luke looked to the ground again.

"Traded for a crossbow? You don't have anything valuable enough to make anyone—oh hell, no. You traded my father's sword for it, didn't you? That's why I didn't see the blade in the bedchamber."

"It's the only thing the huntsman wanted."

"That wasn't yours to trade," Hunter scolded.

"I thought you gave it to Luke," said Regina, getting a scowl from Hunter.

"Yes, but as a family heirloom," Hunter told her. "I wanted him to keep it, not trade it away. It was to stay in our family."

"In his defense, you didn't tell him that. Did you?" asked Regina.

Now it was Hunter's turn to look in the other direction. "Well, not exactly."

"Luke, this still doesn't explain how you got a hold of Lady Sage's brooch." Regina tried to be gentle to coax the truth from the boy.

"I told you. I didn't steal it."

"Who did?" asked Hunter.

Luke remained quiet. Finally he answered. "I don't know who stole it. Fred told me he found it on the ground in the stables and asked me to hold on to it."

"That's a lie," snapped Hunter.

"Mayhap not." Regina stepped in before another argument took place. "It could be possible that the thief really did drop it and Fred found it, just like Luke says."

"Where did he find it exactly and who had been there who could have possibly dropped it?" asked Hunter.

"I don't know." Luke shrugged. "Fred didn't say, but he probably doesn't know either. There are a lot of people who go through the stables during a day."

"You need to ask Fred about it," said Hunter.

"Why? Are you going to accuse Fred of being a thief and

throw him in the dungeon?" Luke shot daggers from his eyes at Hunter.

"Well, if need be, then yes," said Hunter. "I can't let a thief walk free." Hunter wasn't letting up with the boy and Regina realized it was probably because his father had been tough with him as well. Still, this wasn't really working.

"Mayhap we can use this to find the real thief." Regina took the brooch out of her pocket and looked at it in thought. "As bait."

"Yes," said Hunter. "Mayhap Luke can try to trade it for something else and see who wants it."

"Wait. You want me to gamble and bluff again? I'm confused." Luke scratched his head.

"Forget the idea," said Hunter. "It was a bad one. Too dangerous, and besides, I don't want Luke to lie anymore. "Luke, look." Hunter sat back down and leaned forward to talk with the boy. "I know you're not a thief and that you want friends your own age, I understand that. But you need to know that Fred might turn out being a thief if you don't help him go down the right path."

"What do you mean?" asked Luke.

"Don't let him or anyone talk you into doing something that in your heart you don't feel is right. And if Fred doesn't know wrong from right, then you help him decipher it. Understand?"

"So I should help Fred be a better person?" Luke seemed touched that Hunter wasn't accusing him or shunning him anymore.

"Do you think you can do it?" asked Hunter.

"I know I can." For the first time since they'd entered the mews Luke was smiling.

"All right then, no more bluffing," Hunter told him. "Now, we have a thief to catch, you and me and we need to get to work."

"What will we do about the brooch and the crossbow?" asked Regina. "If we tell anyone they've been found, they'll want to know more details. They'll need to know that you've caught the thief, Hunter."

"We're not going to do anything about those things right now," said Hunter. "First, we'll catch the thief. Then, we'll deal with the rest of it. I think since one bird went missing, it is a good bet the thief will try again. Mayhap even tonight. Then he'll most likely be in a big hurry to pawn them off somewhere to get his money."

"I don't like the sound of that," said Regina, feeling her nerves shake at the thought of losing another bird.

"Don't worry. I have a plan," Hunter assured her.

"Well, what should I do with the brooch for now?" she asked.

"Give it back to Luke," Hunter told her.

"What?" Regina blinked, not sure she'd heard him correctly.

"Luke, I want you to put the brooch back in the trunk in our chamber, but make sure you don't tell anyone it's there. Keep the crossbow and boots there as well. It should be a safe hiding place for now since the thief won't think of looking there."

Regina fingered the brooch in hesitation. As much as she wanted to trust in Hunter and this plan, she didn't want the expensive brooch to disappear again.

"It's all right, sweetheart." Hunter reached out and

touched her on the arm. "You can trust Luke and you can trust me. Now give the pin to the boy."

"Yes," she said, nodding her head. "I do trust you, Hunter." Then she looked over at Luke and flashed a smile, handing him the brooch. "I trust you, too, Luke."

"We'll find the thief, Lady Regina." Luke stood up taller and prouder and nodded toward Hunter. "And we'll bring back Lightning for you too, don't you worry. Right, Uncle?"

Hunter looked up in surprise when the boy called him Uncle and Regina realized they had just mended the bond between them. Then Hunter smiled at Luke and nodded back. "Like we always do, son." He stood up and put his arm around Luke's shoulders. "Like we always do."

CHAPTER 15

Regina couldn't sleep that night, being so worried about Lightning as well as the rest of her birds. She tossed and turned so much that she finally decided it was senseless to lie there any longer. She got up in the middle of the night and dressed, meaning to go check on her birds. Roger had offered to stay in the mews overnight since she didn't trust that Cassian would hear the thief if he should come back again for another bird. Sadly, Hunter told her no. He said it would only scare the thief away and he needed to put out bait to catch him. He told her to trust him because he had a plan.

"I won't let my birds be used as bait. Why did I ever let Hunter convince me that this was a good idea? I should have brought the birds to my chamber to sleep with me here," she spoke to herself, wondering now why she hadn't. As much as she wanted to give Hunter free reign with whatever plan he had, she still felt like it was only putting her birds at risk. Nay, she had to protect Hera, Dewdrop, and Cloud. They were like her children and she would never abandon a child. Regina put on a cloak and lit a candle, hurrying from her room.

It was dark in the castle with an occasional wall torch mounted on a sconce every so often. It only gave enough light to see the ground, not to mention the mice that scurried to and fro. "Well, now I know where to get some mice for my birds," she mumbled. Everything was silent in an eerie sort of way. She realized that everyone was sleeping. This was probably the time when the thief wandered about stealing whatever he could get in his sticky hands.

She made her way out of the keep and across the courtyard, not seeing the night guards atop the battlements. Something seemed amiss. For her own peace of mind, she needed to check on Hera, Cloud, and Dewdrop. She couldn't stand the thought of someone stealing another one of her birds. Her heart still ached for Lightning, making her feel like she wanted to retch. She couldn't even imagine possibly never seeing her sweet peregrine falcon again. Hope swelled within her, wanting to believe that Hunter and Luke could really could find the bird before it was too late. She needed to have faith because without it, she would have nothing left to cling to.

Regina pulled open the door of the mews, the bells atop the door jangling softly. Still, she did not even hear a peep from her babies within. Odd, since they usually sensed her approaching. When they heard the bells over the door and knew someone entered, they usually at least fidgeted atop their perches. Her heart thumped hard against her chest as her eyes scanned the area, trying to locate her birds with only the light of the lone candle in her hand. Then she spied three stiff forms atop the perches. Usually her birds flapped their wings when she entered the mews and made little noises of anticipation. Tonight, they were as still as corpses.

She stepped forward and gasped when someone pulled her to the side and clamped their hand over her mouth.

"Keep quiet, Ladybird. Or you'll ruin the plan."

Relief rushed through her when she realized it was only Hunter. He'd dismissed the idea of Roger spending the night in the mews because he'd obviously planned on staying here himself. Hunter blew out her candle and pulled her into the corner of the mews, hunkering down with her in the pitch black.

"What's going on?" she whispered.

"If I'm correct, we are about to catch a thief," he whispered back.

"I hope so." She waited in the dark with Hunter, but nothing was happening. They stayed there for what seemed like at least an hour before she decided she really needed to go and comfort her birds. As she started to speak, Hunter held up his finger to her lips.

"Listen," he whispered.

"I don't hear anything." As soon as she said it, she did hear something. It was the sound of metal clinking. If she wasn't mistaken, she knew this sound. "It's a cage. Someone is here to steal another bird."

"Wait for it," he told her with his hand on her arm.

Sure enough, she saw the door to Cassian's attached room open. The man walked out with not one, but two cages in his hands. He balanced a lit candle in a jar atop them.

"What is he doing?" she whispered.

"Shhh." Hunter held up his hand to keep her quiet.

Cassian put down the cages and then turned back to most likely get another cage from his room. Horror swept through Regina. The man was taking the birds somewhere and she had not given him permission to do so.

The door to the mews opened, the bell above the door jangling softly as when she'd entered. Cassian had his back to the main entrance but when the bells sounded, he looked up and turned around.

"He heard it," she whispered, shocked and not understanding this at all.

"It's about time you came. I told you to be here an hour ago," complained Cassian. "What took so long?"

"I had to make sure that damned thief-taker went to bed first," grumbled the voice of another man. "I waited for a while after I saw him enter the keep, just to be sure he wouldn't return."

Regina realized that Hunter must have sneaked back out here when no one was watching.

"We'll have to move quickly. I want to take all three of them out of here tonight," instructed Cassian.

Regina gasped. Hunter quickly clamped a hand over her mouth.

"Did you hear something?" Cassian looked around.

"Nay. I didn't hear nothing," said the man in the cloak who had entered through the front door. He held up a lantern and looked around. Hunter covered Regina with his body, keeping them hidden in the shadows.

"It's probably the damned birds," grumbled Cassian. "Lately, they don't even want me to touch them, the stupid things."

"I don't like this idea," said the man in the cloak. "Stealing birds from nobles is a crime punishable by death. This is was never part of my plan."

"Nay, but it is my plan exactly and you cannot object unless you want me to turn you in."

"You wouldn't do that."

"Wouldn't I?" asked Cassian. "It was a stroke of luck when you dropped that brooch and I found it."

"I want the brooch back. Where is it? That is worth a lot of money."

Cassian paused before he answered. "I don't know. I lost it."

"Damn you! That would have brought me good coin. Enough to live on for a long time."

"Don't worry, you simpkin. We don't even need the jewelry. These birds will bring in more than enough. We'll be living like kings for the rest of our lives." Cassian slipped the falconer's glove onto his hand. "Have you got the horse and cart waiting?"

"Yes, it's ready."

"What about the night guards? Did you take care of them?"

"Yes. I spiked their ale with bitter nightshade. We'll have a few hours before they are back to normal."

"What? Why didn't you use the hemlock like I told you?" spat Cassian.

"Because, I know that could kill them and I don't want anyone to die. I can't believe you used it on Roger."

"Yes, and I used a good amount, too. That boy must have an iron stomach to have healed so quickly. The amount I gave him should have killed him." Cassian chuckled lowly.

So that's why Roger was sick, Regina realized. It had been foul play to keep him away from the mews. She wanted to strangle Cassian for admitting that he'd tried to kill the boy. She was only thankful that she'd told Sage about Roger being ill before they left for the hunt. Sage was a healer and she must have had a hand in curing him.

"I can't believe they didn't put a guard on the mews," said the mystery man.

"Naw. I convinced them that I'd watch over the birds better."

"Even though they think you can't hear?"

"They're stupid, the lot of them. I could convince them of anything. Come here and hold the cage while I put the birds inside."

Regina wasn't about to let anyone steal her birds, no matter what plan Hunter may have. Not able to sit there and do nothing any longer, she jumped up and made her presence known.

"Stop!" she cried. "Leave my birds alone, you thieves."

"Regina, nay," she heard Hunter groan from behind her.

Before she knew what was happening, the stranger in the cloak grabbed her and held a blade to her throat.

"Release her!" Hunter jumped up with his sword at the ready, but stopped when he saw in the dim light that the thief had Regina and was pressing the sharp edge of a dagger to her throat.

"Drop the sword," warned the man in the cloak. His face was hidden and Hunter couldn't see his identity.

"All right. Just don't hurt her." Hunter threw down his sword.

"Dammit, these aren't even real birds!" spat Cassian, ripping the stuffed image of a bird from the perch that Hunter and Luke had made from covering old shoes with leather and feathers, similar to the way Regina had constructed the birds' lure for training. "We were set up. Damn it, let's get out of here anon." Cassian hurried toward the door. As the man in the cloak pulled Regina out of the mews with him, Hunter reached into his boot to retrieve his throwing dagger. He saw Cassian pull a sharp blade from under his cloak and lunge for Hunter. Hunter raised his knife, struggling with Cassian to free the blade from the man's hand. In the struggle Cassian tripped and fell against Hunter. Hunter raised his arms to protect himself and his blade stuck right into the man's chest. Cassian fell to the ground with blood streaming from his mouth.

Hunter bent down and turned the man over, seeing his bulging eyes. "Where are they taking her?" he bellowed.

"I'll never...tell you...Mercenary." The man died with his eyes open.

"Damn it!" swore Hunter, not meaning to kill the man. He'd been hoping to get information as well as a confession out of him. Now, his only hope was to find Regina's abductor on his own. Hunter retrieved his sword and ran out into the courtyard, looking around for the man who took Regina.

"Hunter," he heard a muffled cry, and looked across the courtyard to see Regina struggling with the man who had taken her. They were disappearing behind the keep. He realized they were probably headed for the postern door as a means of escape. He'd heard the man say there was a horse and cart waiting. The castle's drawbridge was up and the gate down. He had to move quickly if he was going to save Regina.

"Lower the drawbridge," he shouted, but remembered hearing the abductor say that the night guards had been poisoned so they wouldn't be able to help him. "Damn!" he spat, taking off on foot after Regina. Sure enough, when he got to the postern gate, it was open. He was still far from it but could see a horse and cart outside the exit with someone waiting in it.

He darted to the postern gate and crossed through just as the wagon lurched and started to move with two people and Regina inside. Hunter wasn't about to let someone take or possibly kill the woman he loved. He ran after the wagon, diving for the back of it. He caught it, but his sword went clattering to the ground.

"Faster!" cried the man in back still holding onto Regina. Hunter pulled himself up into the wagon as it bumped and jostled back and forth. Once inside the wagon, he dove for the man, managing to knock the knife out of his hand. He pushed Regina to the side for her own safety and punched the man in the face.

"Save yourself, Regina. Jump off the wagon, now." Hunter continued to fight and struggle with her abductor. The man was stronger than Hunter had thought he'd be.

"Nay! I won't let anyone get away with stealing my bird," said Regina, making Hunter realize that she wasn't about to listen to him. Why should he be surprised?

• • •

Regina was determined to help Hunter catch her abductors, and the last thing she was going to do was to jump off the wagon and leave Hunter alone with two of the thieves. As Hunter and the man fought, she made her way to the front of the wagon, holding on to the side as the cart as it bounced back and forth over the rugged terrain.

She lifted one leg and crawled over the side of the wagon onto the driver's seat. The driver looked over at her and she realized it was a woman. Somehow, that gave her even more confidence. She made a fist and swung, hitting the woman in the mouth. The driver fell off the wagon, and the horse ran wild pulling the cart with it.

"Oh, no!" she cried, trying to reach for the reins but she just couldn't get them. She looked over her shoulder to see Hunter and her abductor still fighting in back of the wagon. When she looked back at the horse, in the moonlight she saw a big hole in the road approaching fast. "Nay!" she cried. The wagon hit the hole, busting a wheel and causing the cart to be half-dragged. The horse continued to run, pulling them behind it. She fell forward and thankfully managed to grab the reins. With one yank, she yelled out. "Whoa! Whoa!"

When the horse stopped and the wagon settled, she looked back to realize that Hunter and her abductor must have fallen out. She jumped from the wagon and ran back to lend her help. That's when she saw Hunter on the ground on top of the man, holding the man's hands behind his back. He clasped the thief's wrists with iron shackles.

Hunter looked up at her and his eyes opened wide. "Regina, behind you!"

She turned to find the woman driver raising a large rock

above her head. Regina tried to cover her head but was too late. The rock came down hard, smashing into her skull. Regina's head throbbed with pain and she felt blood leaking down the back of her neck. Then, everything went black in front of her eyes. Her legs went limp and she hit the ground, unconscious.

CHAPTER 16

Regina awoke with the worst headache of her life. She blinked several times, realizing she was no longer on the road but back in her own bed and had no idea how she'd gotten here. The last thing she remembered was one of her abductors hitting her over the head with a rock.

"Hunter?" she muttered, still half asleep.

"I'm here, Ladybird." She rolled onto her back and looked up to see the smiling, handsome face of Hunter staring down at her with a concerned look in his brown eyes. He sat down on the edge of the bed and reached out to take her hand.

"How long have you been here?" she asked, noticing light streaming in through the window.

"It's been two days now, sweetheart. But I would have stayed here two years if need be."

"The thieves!" She tried to sit up, but felt pain in her head and a dizziness overtake her.

"Take it slow," Hunter told her. "Now, lay back down.

You've had a bad blow to the head and are lucky to be alive at all."

"Yes. I remember now." Her hand went to the back of her head. "I have stitches, don't I?"

"You do. Sage is to thank for that. She used her healing herbs on you and did a wonderful job sewing up the wound. She said you should be fine in a few days if you ever awake, and you have."

The door to the room opened and Sage came in carrying a tray of jars that looked to contain healing creams. "You're awake!" Sage blurted out. Leaving the door open, Sage hurried to Regina's bedside.

"Sage, thank you so much," said Regina. "You too, Hunter." She gripped his hand in hers. "Because of you two I'm still alive."

"We can't say the same for Cassian." Robin walked into the room with Roger. "Hunter killed him in the mews."

"Oh," said Regina, not having known the man had died.

"I didn't mean to kill him," said Hunter. "I just didn't want him to get away. It was an unfortunate accident and he died in the struggle."

"I cannot believe Cassian was the thief." Regina tried to clear her head.

"He could also hear just fine and was faking it all along," Hunter explained.

"Why? Why would he do that?" Regina felt perplexed about the actions of the man.

"If I may cut in?" Roger stepped forward. Robin nodded. "Lady Regina, Cassian felt very hurt when you took over his position as master falconer. I think he wanted revenge on not only you but on Robin and everyone new who came to Shrewsbury Castle after the death of the last lord."

"Who were his accomplices? It was a woman who hit me." Regina's hand went to her head.

"Don't touch the stitches. I have balms to use that will help you heal." Sage opened a jar. "It was my handmaid, Clotilda, who stole my brooch. She confessed to taking it. It seems somehow Cassian discovered the fact and took the brooch and then lost it."

"That is when Fred and Luke found it," said Hunter. "Just like my nephew said."

"Who was the thief who held a knife to my throat?" Regina felt sick to her stomach just remembering how frightened she'd been.

"It was the stable groom, Al," Robin told her.

"Al? Oh no," groaned Regina, having liked the man.

"It seems he and Clotilda were a couple in secret. They'd planned on stealing just enough to sell and make them money to live on. They were going to leave the castle and start over somewhere else and bring Fred with them."

"They didn't like me getting the title of Lord Shrewsbury either, it seems," said Robin, looking like he felt dejected.

"I am guessing that horse pulling the wagon last night was the stolen one from Sir Elwood?" asked Regina.

"Yes," answered Robin. "Since Al had access to all the horses and wagons in the stable, it was easy for him to sneak them out. However, now Sir Elwood's horse has been returned."

"Luke also gave back the boots and crossbow to the guards he'd swindled them from," Hunter told her. "I am happy to say Father's sword has been returned as well."

"That's good," she said, her throat so dry she could barely talk. There was one more missing thing that no one seemed to be mentioning. It was a question she had to ask but was afraid to do so because of the answer she might hear. Still, she had to know. It was the most important question of all. "Please, someone tell me that Lightning has been found and that she is not harmed at all."

No one said a word. That told her all she needed to hear. Regina closed her eyes, wanting to die. She couldn't even imagine life without her bird.

"Hera, Dewdrop, and Cloud are in the mews waiting for you," Roger told her. "They were never in any real danger."

"That's right," said Hunter. "At the last minute, Luke and I decided to exchange the birds with fake ones, knowing the thief would return."

"I kept your birds in Lord Hunter's bedchamber overnight with me," explained Roger. "They were never in any danger."

"Thank you, but why didn't anyone think to tell me this before?" asked Regina. "They are my birds and I needed to know."

"It was late and you were already sleeping when we came up with the plan," said Hunter. "We didn't want to wake you since you were so distraught about Lightning."

"Did anyone even bother to look for Lightning? We have to find her. Did the thieves tell you where to find her?" Regina pushed up to a sitting position in the bed.

"We're still working on that," said Hunter. "Neither Al or Clotilda know where she is being kept. They said Cassian took the bird somewhere. They never wanted to be involved with stealing the hunting birds to begin with, but Cassian was blackmailing them to go along with him."

"Since Cassian is now dead, that means so is Lightning." Regina wanted to cry. "I will never see my baby again."

"Not so," came a voice from the door.

Regina looked up to see Luke in the doorway holding a cage with a bird in it.

"Lightning!" she cried, starting to get out of bed. "She's alive!"

"Nay, you stay put." Hunter held her down, insistent that she didn't move.

"Is she all right? Bring her to me." Regina held out her hands. Luke walked over and held up the cage and Regina peeked in at her bird. "You poor thing. I am so sorry, Lightning. I will never let that happen again."

"She seems fine," said Roger, walking over to inspect the bird through the cage. "I'll tend to the falcon and feed her and make sure she has not been injured."

"Thank you, Roger." Regina lay back on the pillow smiling, releasing a deep breath of relief. Roger took the cage from Luke, leaving the room with the bird.

"Luke, how did you find the bird?" asked Hunter. "Robin and his men searched everywhere for it."

"I had a little help." Luke nodded at the door. Fred was standing there, almost as if he were afraid to enter.

"Fred? You?" asked Hunter.

"Fred and I went out looking for Lightning as well," said Luke. "We heard a jingling noise, like from a bell. We followed it and that is when we found Lightning in the cage tucked away in a cave. She was trying her hardest to get out of the cage and fly away."

"Thank you, Luke and Fred for bringing Lightning back home alive," Regina told them. "I will forever be grateful."

"I didn't know my grandfather was a thief," said Fred in a sheepish manner. "What will happen to him now?"

"That is yet to be decided," Robin answered. "Fred, did you help steal any of the missing items? Tell me the truth."

"Well...no." Fred looked down.

"Fred, it's not good to lie," whispered Luke. "You'd better tell them."

"I found the brooch on the ground in the stables and should have turned it in," admitted Fred. "But I was afraid."

"Why?" asked Robin.

"I guess I had an idea that my grandfather might be stealing things, because I saw him sneaking the guard's horse out of the stable one night. He didn't know I saw him."

"And you couldn't say anything because he was your grandfather?" asked Regina.

"Yes," said the boy sadly. "He is the only family I have."

"We will discuss this later, boys." Hunter looked over to Robin. "I need to speak with Lord Robin about a few things right now."

"I want to go see my birds," said Regina. "I cannot wait."

"Nay. You are going nowhere until I say so," Sage scolded. "You are my patient now and you will stay right here in bed to heal until I tell you otherwise."

"Your birds will be fine, Regina." Hunter picked up her hand and kissed it. "Roger will take good care of them. Plus, I will sleep in the mews each night to watch over them. You will be back to flying and training them soon, I promise."

"Thank you, Hunter. I will feel at ease now." Regina

looked up and smiled, so happy to have not only a man in her life to love, but also the return of Lightning and the safety of all her birds. "Thank you, everyone."

"There is no need for you to sleep in the mews, thief-taker." Robin told Hunter. "I will post a guard or two outside the door at night. Now, come to my solar. I will pay you our agreed upon fee and then you and the boy are free to go."

"To go? Hunter, didn't you tell him?" Regina looked up at him, thinking he looked insecure all of a sudden.

"Tell me what?" asked Robin.

"Lord Robin, I am in love with your sister and I have asked her to marry me," Hunter said with the greatest of ease.

"You what?" Robin was shocked to say the least.

"You heard him," Regina broke in. "We are in love and want to be married as soon as possible."

"Oh, that is wonderful," gushed Sage. "I am so happy for you both. Congratulations."

"Hunter, I think we need to talk. Meet me in my solar in an hour." Robin turned and walked out the door.

Regina's heart fell in her chest. Why was her brother giving her such a hard time? And why did he want to talk to Hunter? This worried her to no end.

"Hunter, I'm coming with you when you speak with my brother," said Regina. "I won't let you face him alone."

"Nay, Regina, it's all right," Hunter assured her. "It is something I have to do by myself. If not, I'll never be able to face my inner demons. You stay here and heal."

"Yes, you're right," Regina agreed. "Although something tells me that you've already rid yourself of those nasty voices in your head."

Hunter knocked on Robin's door an hour later, feeling anxious and extremely on edge. Was the man going to object to him marrying Regina? If so, he'd fight tooth and nail to make her his wife. He paused for a second, taking a moment to organize his thoughts.

That's when he realized the voice of his departed sister was no longer taunting him, making him feel less than worthy. Regina's love is what made that disappear. Regina believed in him and helped him see that true love can make any hate, doubt or feelings of worthlessness diminish.

He raised his fist and knocked, feeling sure of himself. He could face Lord Robin easily now and fight for the woman he loved. Hunter was sure of it.

"Enter," came Robin's voice from within.

Hunter opened the door and stepped inside. And stopped dead in his tracks. It was not only Robin in the room, but also Madoc, Regina's father. His confidence wavered. Hunter half-expected the taunting voice of his sister to return right now, but was glad when it didn't come. Still, he wasn't at all so sure of himself anymore. Sweat beaded on his brow when it wasn't even a hot day.

"Thief-taker, come in and close the door." Madoc cradled a goblet in his hands. "My son tells me there is something we need to discuss."

"Lord Madoc. I didn't expect you to be here." Hunter slowly entered the room and closed the door behind him.

"Robin sent a pigeon with a missive to tell me Regina was hurt and that the thief was caught. There are still things to be done regarding the death of my father-by-marriage, but just the same, I came right away. I've just arrived at the castle and haven't even had time to see my daughter yet."

"Regina will be fine, my lord," said Hunter with a bow of his head. "Lady Sage's expert ministrations have seen to that. Regina has now awoken after two days of being unconscious."

"Good, good. Then I suppose there is no need to call for my wife at this time." Madoc walked closer to Hunter. "Robin tells me you are to thank for catching the thieves and also for saving my daughter."

"All in a day's work, my lord," Hunter answered.

"I am grateful for your skills, Thief-taker. I knew you'd be the perfect one for this job," Madoc continued. "Your father has trained you well."

"Thank you, my lord, but my late father has nothing to do with my skills of being a thief-taker. He taught me to be a mercenary only."

"Stealing from nobles is a great offense. Those thieves will be imprisoned for a long time," stated Madoc.

"Will they be executed?" Hunter never liked anyone being executed if it wasn't truly necessary.

"That is up to my son, Robin." Madoc looked over to his son.

"I haven't decided their punishment yet," Robin told them. "However, they weren't the ones to steal the falcon. That was Cassian only. That would have been a death sentence for sure if you hadn't already seen to that for me, Hunter."

"Glad I could be of help," muttered Hunter.

"In regards to the handmaid, her sentence will be lighter than the stable groom," said Robin in thought. "Al, however threated Regina's life. On second thought, he might have to die after all."

"The stable groom has a grandson, doesn't he?" asked Madoc.

"Yes," said Robin. "His name is Fred. But he wasn't part of the thieving. However, he did know about it so that makes him guilty as well."

"I believe Fred didn't actually know for sure, but just had suspicions," Hunter corrected him. "What will happen to the boy? He doesn't have anyone to care for him at all anymore."

"The boy is thirteen," Robin pointed out.

"Yes, that is old enough to fend for himself." Madoc took a sip of wine. "Will you keep him working in the stables, Robin?"

"I think so," said Robin, pouring a drink for himself. "Without Al, I'll need all the help in the stables that I can get. However, I would feel better if someone kept an eye on Fred. Just in case we can't trust him after all."

"I'll do it," Hunter offered, seeming to surprise both Robin and Madoc.

"You?" Madoc looked at Hunter and then over to his son.

"Yes, I will watch over him and make certain he stays on the right path," Hunter assured them. "My nephew, Luke has become good friends with the boy. Perhaps Lord Robin will consider taking Luke on as a stableboy as well? He has been spending a lot of time there and is a fast learner."

"Interesting that you made that offer." Madoc took another drink. "That would mean you'd have to stay at Shrewsbury Castle. With your job, how would that work?"

"Well, my lord." Hunter cleared his throat. "As I have

already told Lord Robin, your daughter Regina and I have fallen in love."

Madoc almost choked on his wine. "What did you say?"

"I have asked Regina to marry me and she has accepted." Hunter blurted it out before he had time to lose his nerve.

"She has, has she?" Madoc's stern look interlocked with Robin's. "Son, you didn't think to mention this to me?"

"I only just heard about it myself, Father," answered Robin with a shrug.

Hunter spoke up once again. "Lord Madoc, I would ask for your approval and your blessing to make your daughter my wife."

"I see." Madoc didn't look all that happy with the idea.

"Regina swears she loves him," Robin interjected. "Even though Hunter is a commoner, do remember that Sage was a commoner as well when I married her."

"You don't need to remind me," muttered Madoc.

"Thank you, Lord Robin," said Hunter with a nod, surprised that the man would stick up for him. Then he spoke again to Madoc. "Lord Madoc, you were the one who called me here to Shrewsbury Castle. You trusted me enough to get the job done, and I don't believe I have let you done."

"Nay. Nay, you haven't," agreed Madoc.

"I also know that you admired my father, even though he was not noble."

"Your father saved my life," said Madoc.

"Hunter saved Regina's life as well," Robin pointed out, being more of a godsend than Hunter could even have imagined.

Madoc looked down to his goblet, swirling the contents

as he responded. "Even if I didn't think so at first, your father, Robert did prove to be a good man in the end."

"Thank you, my lord," said Hunter. "I will be a good husband to Regina. I promise you that I will be even a better man than my father."

"I see." Madoc put down the cup and paced the floor, not saying a word. Then he stopped and walked back to Hunter. "I know how you feel, Hunter. I was once naught but a thief before I discovered that I was truly a noble. Therefore, I can see both sides of the situation here."

"Then you'll give me your approval and your blessing to marry your daughter?"

"This is really what Regina wants?" Madoc looked up, squinting one eye.

"It is, my lord. It is what we both want." Hunter held his breath waiting for his answer.

"Father, it is what Regina told us just an hour ago, I assure you," agreed Robin, coming to Hunter's rescue once again.

"She was in her right mind at the time?" asked Madoc. "I mean, she did take a hard blow to the head."

"She was sane," Hunter assured him. "Although, I have to admit that I am still a little in awe that I am the one she wants to marry."

That made them all laugh.

"Robin, give this man some wine so we can celebrate," instructed Madoc.

"Celebrate?" asked Hunter, needing more of a definite answer.

Madoc walked over and picked up his goblet and held it high in the air. "Hunter Chase, you have my approval as well as my blessing to marry my daughter, Regina. Welcome to the family. But I must warn you, that you have no idea what you're getting yourself into."

"Thank you, my lord. I will welcome whatever is thrown my way," said Hunter, taking his cup from Robin and holding it high as well. "I have never been happier in my life than I am right now. Thank you, both. I am honored to be part of your family."

CHAPTER 17
TWO DAYS LATER

"Go on, boys. You know what you have to do." Hunter helped Regina out of the wagon, having stopped in front of the tailor's shop in town. Luke and Fred were in the back of the wagon. Luke clutched Inky in his arms.

"I don't want to give up my cat," whined Luke.

"Whose cat?" Hunter gave the boys a nasty stare.

"William's cat," said Luke sadly, scooting out of the wagon. Fred did the same.

"Hunter, can't we just buy the cat from William?" asked Regina.

"We could, but we won't." Hunter shook his head. "The boys are in my care now, and I can't let them get away with stealing."

"They said the cat followed them home," Regina tried once again.

"With a lot of coaxing," Hunter answered, pulling open the door. "Let's go, boys. There is a lot of planning to do for the wedding and we need to get back to the castle quickly."

"Yes, Uncle," said Luke, slowly entering the building, clutching on to Inky.

"Yes, Uncle," repeated Fred, following his friend inside.

Regina grabbed onto Hunter's arm. "Did Fred just call you...Uncle?"

"Yes," said Hunter, looking extremely pleased. "He asked if he could call me that since I am now his guardian. I think it is because he admires Luke and my nephew has started calling me Uncle again instead of Hunter."

"That makes you happy, doesn't it?" Regina felt so happy with everything that she couldn't stop smiling.

"It does," he admitted. "But not half as happy that tomorrow, you and I will be wed and you will be my wife." He bent over and kissed her on the mouth.

"I still think you're being a little too hard on the boys. Luke loves that cat and will do anything for her."

"I know. Did you see how fat the cat's become? I think Luke has been feeding her way too much."

They entered the shop and were greeted by both William and his wife, Bernadette.

"Regina, you're all right, thank goodness." Bernadette ran to Regina, giving her a big hug. "We heard what happened and we were so frightened for you."

"Thank you, Aunt Bernadette," Regina answered. "Because of Hunter and Sage's ministrations, I feel just about back to normal."

"Hello," said Hunter to the couple with a nod of his head.

"I hear congratulations are in order," said William. "So, the wedding is tomorrow at the castle?"

"Yes," answered Hunter. "Regina and I decided we didn't want to wait."

"Mother, Dot, and Martine are coming, but we decided to keep it a small gathering," Regina told them. "You'll be there, though, won't you?"

"We wouldn't miss it for the world," said William. "Besides, I don't see my brother, Madoc, that much anymore and cherish visiting with him. Since this is such short notice, I don't suppose you have a wedding gown, do you?"

"Nay," answered Regina. "It doesn't matter. I'll just wear a nice gown."

"No, you won't." William walked over to the worktable, holding up a beautiful gown made of blue velvet. It was trimmed in an ornate burgundy satin with white lacing at the bodice. "I've been working on this gown, and I'd like you to have it. As a present from us for your big day."

"Really?" Regina walked up and gently ran her fingers over the soft cloth. "It is so beautiful, Uncle William, I love it. However, I am sure it is for another noble."

"Nay, it isn't. It is just something I wanted to construct, hoping some beautiful woman would want to wear it someday."

"I do," she said, with wide eyes. "I would be honored to wear such a fine creation at my wedding."

"Then it's yours," said William. "I'll come to the castle later today for your final fitting. Oh, and I will make up a quick wedding tunic for you as well, Hunter."

"Thank you. That is kind of you." Hunter nodded, sounding choked by such kindness.

"Uncle, you are the best." Regina gave William a hug and a kiss.

Hunter cleared his throat. "William, Luke and Fred have something to tell you. Go on, boys."

"We're returning Inky to you." Luke sadly held out the cat and William took her.

"Really? Why?" William's gaze traveled over to Hunter.

"Fred? Did you want to tell him?" asked Hunter.

"Yes, sir." Fred let out a deep sigh and looked at the floor when he spoke. "We stole your cat and we're sorry."

"I always wanted a black cat and so we coaxed her with lots of food until she followed us home," admitted Luke.

"I see," chuckled William, petting the cat in his arms. "Well, this cat is good at catching mice, and I'd hate to lose her."

"William, let the boys have the cat. We can get another one," said Bernadette softly.

"Nay, I cannot allow the boys to get away with thinking they can take whatever they want," protested Hunter. "I'm afraid this is a hard lesson that they're going to just have to learn."

"I agree," said William. "Stealing is not an admirable trait. I learned that many years ago. However, I would like to make a deal."

"A deal?" asked Luke. "What kind of deal?"

"If you boys want to work in my shop for the next few weeks sweeping up and doing a few other chores, you can visit with Inky. Anytime you want, actually. I'll also make sure you each end up with a cat of your own very soon. Cats that are earned, not stolen."

"Uncle, what are you saying?" asked Regina.

"Did any of you notice how fat this cat has become?" William rubbed the cat's belly.

"I'm afraid Luke must have gotten a little overzealous in feeding her," answered Hunter.

"Mayhap so, but this cat is pregnant and about to give birth soon."

"She is?" Luke's eyes opened wide.

"Then there are going to be lots of kittens?" asked Fred with a huge smile.

"Yes," chuckled William. "More than I can use in this little shop. Therefore, you boys are both welcome to choose a kitten of your own when they are old enough to leave their mother."

"Can we?" both the boys asked at once, looking over at Hunter.

"If you work off your debt at the shop, then I don't see why not," Hunter answered.

"We have a lot of mice in the castle," Regina told William. "If you have any extra cats, the castle could always use them. I might even be able to train the cats to bring the mice to me to feed the rodents to my birds."

"You've got it," answered William with a chuckle.

"So, Hunter. You and Luke will be living at the castle from now on?" asked Regina's aunt.

"Aye," Hunter answered. "Lord Robin and Lady Sage were kind enough to welcome us into their home."

"I'm going to be a stableboy with Fred," Luke proudly announced.

"Really? That's great," said William. "Hunter, will you still be needing your house in the woods? If not, my daughter and her husband are looking for a place to live since it is getting crowded here with so many people."

"I'd be happy to make negotiations with you after the

wedding." Hunter put his arm around Regina. "After all, I am starting a new life as a married man, and I think I'd like to rid myself of everything from my past. So, this will be perfect."

"Will you still be a thief-taker?" Bernadette wondered.

"Nay," said Hunter. "I have decided that those days are behind me now."

"Hunter will have the courtesy title of Lord once we're married," explained Regina.

"What will you be doing at the castle?" asked William.

"Well, I'm not sure yet."

Regina noticed how uncomfortable Hunter felt and her heart went out to him. She wanted the best for him and his new life. "Robin offered the position of castle guard to Hunter, but Hunter turned him down."

"Why?" asked William. "You are a skilled protector and fighter. It would be a perfect job for you."

"I'm tired of fighting," said Hunter. "I want a true skill. An admirable skill like my wife-to-be has."

"Good thing," said Regina. "Because I will be needing another trainee in the mews now that Cassian is gone."

"Regina? What are you saying?" asked Hunter. "You still have Roger."

"Yes, but I plan on getting a few more birds. Therefore, I will need more help in the mews. Hunter, I think you would be perfect for the job."

"Me?" He looked to be in shock.

"Thank you, sweetheart, but I know nothing about birds."

"That's not true," she protested. "I've already been training you and I can tell that the birds like you."

"You can tell, huh?" He didn't seem as if he believed her.

"I would like to work with my husband. What is wrong with that?"

"If you don't take the offer, you may never see your wife," said William. "Regina spends way too much time with those birds."

"Well, I do see your point," said Hunter with a chuckle. "We can't be newlyweds and never be together."

"Then you'll accept the position of falconer's apprentice?" asked Regina.

"Mayhap," said Hunter. "I mean, yes. Yes, I would like that," he said with newfound confidence. "With you as my teacher, I have nothing to fear."

"Perfect." Regina took Hunter's head in her hands and kissed him passionately right there in front of everyone. "Now, let's get home because we need to get ready for our wedding."

CHAPTER 18

"Regina, everyone is waiting in the courtyard. It is time," said Regina's mother, Abbey. Today was Regina's wedding day and she couldn't be happier.

"You are so lucky to be getting married to a man you love." Her sister, Dot wove red roses into the braid that encircled Regina's head. She made sure to cover the stitches with a flower so no one could see them. Regina wore the wedding gown that her uncle had made her, feeling prettier than she ever had before. It made her feel like a queen.

"Martine, let's go take our seats," said Abbey, reaching out for Regina's older sister's hand.

"Good luck, Sister," said Regina, blowing her a kiss. "I'm sure you and Hunter will be as happy and David and me. And I'm sure you'll be starting a family soon as well." Martine rubbed her belly, being seven months pregnant. "Just like Robin and also most of our cousins. Our family is really growing."

"Oh, Mother, now I feel bad that we didn't wait longer to get married, and invite all the cousins as well," said Regina, feeling a nervous fluttering in her belly.

"I wouldn't worry about that," said her mother. "Things always turn out the way they were meant to be."

"I hear the music of the musicians. We'd better hurry and take our seats." Martine pulled her mother out the door.

"It's time," said Dot, picking up a bouquet of red roses and handing it to Regina. She was Regina's bridesmaid today.

"I'm nervous," Regina admitted. "I just want everything to go smoothly today."

"It will." Dot put her hand on Regina's back and guided her to the door. "Just remember who you're marrying and that should put all your fears at ease."

"Yes. You're right." Regina smiled. "I am marrying the man I love and that makes everything perfect."

When Regina got to the courtyard, she stopped. "Why are there so many people here?" she asked, seeing the crowd below. "I thought we were keeping it a small ceremony."

"They all wanted to be here to help you celebrate," Dot told her.

"All? All who?"

"Look closer, Sister. Robin sent a messenger pigeon to all our cousins."

"They're here." Regina smiled, happy that they had come, after all. "Are they all here?"

"All but Lark and the MacKeefes. There wasn't enough time for them to travel here from the Highlands, but they were informed."

"I'll have to make certain to thank Robin for this."

Regina walked toward the archway made of flowers where she would take her vows. Dot followed, straightening out her long burgundy cloak that trailed behind her, brushing over the cobbled stones. The music sounded beautiful. Musicians played flutes, harps, lutes and even a hurdy-gurdy. She nodded to her cousins, aunts and uncles as she made her way to the man she loved.

Regina was especially happy to see her cousin Eleanor and her husband Connor with their baby, Elizabeth, who had been born in January. Eleanor's brother, Edgar, or Gar, as they all called him, stood with his wife, Josefina, cradling their newborn son, Eliot, in his big arms. They were the children of Madoc's twin sister, Echo. The family all seemed to have a lot of names starting with E and it didn't look like it would be stopping anytime soon.

She approached the arch and the music softened and then stopped all together. Her eyes fastened to Hunter looking so handsome in his new clothes that William had constructed for him. Clothes of a noble, but not too ornate since Hunter still had trouble accepting that he'd be a lord from this day on. Luke served as his best man, holding the rings tied to a small velvet pillow that William had supplied as well.

"Regina," said Hunter taking her hands in his. "You are beautiful."

"And you are so handsome," was her reply.

They said their vows and before she knew it, she was a married woman.

"Throw the bouquet," called out Dot, wanting more than anything to catch it.

"All right." Regina turned around and threw the flowers

over her shoulder. She heard laughing and when she turned around she could see why. "Evan? You caught the flowers?" Evan was the brother of Eleanor and Edgar and also the only one in his family not yet married.

"Nay! Dot did." He threw the bouquet to Dot. The girl's frown turned to a quick smile.

"Regina, there are a lot of people here that I don't know," Hunter whispered.

"Don't worry, I will introduce you to them all. There is my cousin, Raven, and her husband, Jonathon." She waggled her fingers at them. Over there is her twin brother, Rook, and his wife, Rose. Plus, Tolin, their brother just got married at Christmas and is here with his wife, Kit." She spied all the baked goods spread out in a beautiful array on a nearby table. "Oh, it looks like Kit made some lovely treats. She's a baker, you know."

"I see."

Uncle Corbett and Aunt Devon are their parents. They're right over there," she said, pointing. "Daegel, their other son isn't married yet but he's about to be knighted."

"Regina," said Hunter in a soft voice.

"Then, over there is my Aunt Echo and her husband, Garrett, who is Lord Warden of the Cinque Ports." She raised her hand and waved to them. "Their daughter, Eleanor, and her husband, Conner, just had a baby after Christmas. Plus, their son, Gar, and his wife, Josefina, have a new baby boy."

"Regina," said Hunter once again.

"Evan, their brother just caught the bouquet."

"That is nice they could all be here."

"Oh, they're not all here."

"They're not?" Hunter's words sounded guarded.

"Nay. I have a Scottish uncle named Storm and his wife is my father's sister, Wren. They live in Scotland and couldn't make it here in time with my cousins Lark, Renard, Hawke and Heather."

"Regina, stop it. I'm overwhelmed."

"Oh, did you hear my sister, Martine, is having a baby in a few months and that Dot wants to get married more than ever now?"

Hunter pulled her into his arms and dipped her down, kissing her long and hard.

The crowd cheered and the music started back up.

"You did that to shut me up, didn't you?" she asked with a giggle.

"You think?"

"Lady Regina, we have a surprise for you," said Luke, standing there with Fred. "Actually, you have to come out to the field to see it."

"A surprise?" asked Regina. She looked over at Hunter. "What is this all about?"

"You'll have to go out to the field to see," Hunter repeated.

"All right then. Let's go."

Regina and Hunter led the way to the open field just outside the castle with the procession of guests following right behind them.

"Are those my birds?" Regina spied all four of her birds perched and tethered, awaiting her arrival.

"It wouldn't be right not to have your 'babies' at the wedding, so I made sure they were invited as well," said Hunter, melting her heart by his thoughtful act.

Roger stood with a falconer's glove in his hand awaiting them.

"My lord and lady," he said with a bow.

"I can't believe I'm being called lord," mumbled Hunter. "It is really going to take some time to get used to that."

"You will," said Regina. "Or mayhap I should say, Lord Hunter."

"Are you going to let the birds fly?" asked Luke.

"Why not?" she answered. "But only one at a time."

"Here you are, my lady." Roger handed her the bag of meat.

"I'll take that," said Hunter, slipping the handle of the bag over his shoulder. "We wouldn't want to soil my wife's new dress."

"Actually, I think since you're now my new apprentice that it is a good idea. Give me your hand." Regina reached out for him.

"What?" Hunter looked at her in confusion.

"Give me your hand."

Hunter held out his hand and she slipped the falconer's glove over it.

"Regina? What are you doing?"

"Roger, let's start out with Lightning," she suggested. "I am sure Lightning is happier than any of the birds to be here today since she almost wasn't."

"Aye, my lady." Roger took Lightning off her perch, slipping off the hood that covered her eyes. The bird sat atop his falconer's glove.

"Now, please hand Lightning to Hunter."

"What? Regina, nay. I don't know how to do this," Hunter protested.

"It's time you learn. Besides, Lightning knows what she is doing, don't worry."

"I thought you said the bird has to learn to trust me first. Nay. We can't do this."

"If Lightning sees that I trust you, I am sure she will too." Regina held on to Hunter's hand with the glove and the bird hopped over and perched herself atop it. Regina dug into the pouch at Hunter's side and handed Lightning a piece of raw meat that she gobbled right down.

"This is the most amazing thing ever." Hunter's gaze was fastened on the bird atop his hand. A wide smile lit up his face.

"Now, raise your hand up higher in the air and she'll fly." Regina helped him do it and the falcon took off flying high. The crowed ooed and awed.

"It is so amazing to watch that bird soar," commented Hunter.

"What is even more amazing is seeing the smile on my new apprentice's face," answered Regina. "I am going to call the bird back now. This time, you were give her the treat."

"Me? Nay. You do it."

"Nope. Give me your hand."

"Which hand?"

"The one without the glove, silly." She put a piece of raw meat in his fingers. "Just be sure to hold it at the end when she takes it so you don't accidentally get bit."

"I rather like my fingers," he answered nervously. "I hope to still have them when this is over."

"I am going to call her now." Regina whistled and the bird headed right back toward them. "Hold your gloved hand high and away from your body so she doesn't have to fly too close. We don't want her to hurt herself."

"Like this?" Hunter held his gloved hand high and proud.

"That's right. Now be sure to have her treat ready. She'll want to be rewarded right away."

"Why is this so nerve-wrecking?" asked Hunter. "I've never even felt this nervous while hunting down thieves. Or getting married." He looked at her from the corner of his eye and winked.

"It takes a long time, but you'll learn to relax. You're already proving to be an excellent student, Hunter. Here she comes. Get ready."

The bird landed right on Hunter's glove. Regina took his freewrist and raised it up and Lightning ate the meat right out of Hunter's hand.

"I did it! She did it. This is so amazing," crooned Hunter. "I think I am really going to like being a falconer after all."

"Falconer's apprentice," she teased him and giggled. "Roger, please take Lightning so I can kiss my new husband."

"Yes, my lady." Roger took the bird and Regina reached up and kissed Hunter. His hands, one of them still gloved, went around her waist to pull her closer.

"I think I am going to like working together with you," she told him. "Plus, I already like being married. How about you, Hunter?"

"It is a feeling I cannot describe."

"Try," she teased him once again.

"All right." With his arms still around her, he pursed his mouth and then nodded his head. "I think I have it. It feels honorable, exciting, peaceful, blissful, invigorating and I'd have to say pretty much all around amazing."

"Oh, is that all?" She kissed him again.

"Never," he told her. "I am sure being married to you will hold many surprises and all of them good, my lady, my love, my beautiful, wonderful, amazing **Ladybird**."

FROM THE AUTHOR

I hope you enjoyed Ladybird and will take a moment to leave a review for me.

I have always loved anything to do with falconry. Researching it, I discovered more than I ever knew. There were actually lady falconers back in the medieval times even if they were not the norm. Since I love writing strong heroines, I decided to make my falconer a woman instead of a man.

This book takes place in the 1300s but in 1486 the Boke of St. Albans was written, decreeing what type of nobleman could own which types of birds. For example, gyrfalcons were reserved for kings. A gyrfalcon is the bird you see on the cover of Ladybird. Hawks and falcons and any of the hunting birds were expensive to keep and also one of the reasons that only nobles owned them.

While thief-takers were real, the term wasn't really used

until the 1500s. But, I liked it so much that I used my artistic license to write a thief-taker into my book. It was much like a bounty hunter but the thief-taker was hired by crime victims to catch the thief and return the goods instead of being paid by a bail bondsmen to catch fugitives.

I have been enjoying writing this second generation series (of the Blake family) that deals with nobles falling in love with, and marrying commoners. Of course, that was probably never seen back then, but I like to push the envelope and always ask the question, 'what if?' I also enjoy bringing to life the trades which aren't seen much when books are just about nobles.

Anyway, I thought I had finished this series several books ago, but alas, I was wrong. It seems not only my readers want more, but I still have several of the Blake children (next generation) that want their stories told too. That said, we'll just have to wait and see how many more books come forth.

In the meantime, I am posting the Blake Family Tree of who married whom and who their children are, and the children's children as well. Or at least up until the point we are at the end of this book.

If you'd like to read more about Regina's parents, Madoc and Abbey, you can do so in **Lord of Illusion**, Book 3 of my **Legacy of the Blade Series.** You will also find out Uncle Williams story in that book. If you want to read Regina's brother, Robin's story, you can find it in **Winter Sage**. And her sister, Martine has her romance with the innkeeper David in **Sweet Mead for Lady Martine.**

<u>Here are the books in the Below the Salt Series up until this point:</u>

Below the Salt Series:

Picking up the Gauntlet – Book 1 (Lady Raven is the daughter of Corbett and Devon from Lord of the Blade.)

A Rose Among Thorns – Book 2 (Lord Rook is Raven's twin brother.)

Love Letters for Lady Lark – Book 3 (Lark is the daughter of Storm MacKeefe and Wren from Lady Renegade.)

Dancing on Air – Book 4 (Lady Eleanor is the daughter of Garrett Blackmore and Echo from Lady of the Mist.)

Winter Sage – Book 5 (Lord Robin is the son of Madoc (Echo's twin brother) and Abbey from Lord of Illusion.)

Riding out the Storm – Book 6 (Gar is the son of Echo and stepson/nephew of Garrett from Lady of the Mist.)

Sweet Mead for Lady Martine – Book 7 (Lady Martine is the daughter of Madoc and Abbey from Lord of Illusion.)

Lord of Misrule – Book 8 (Lord Tolin is son of Lord Corbett Blake and Devon from Lord of the Blade.)

Ladybird – Book 9 (Lady Regina is the daughter of Madoc and Abbey from Lord of Illusion.)

If you'd like to know more about my books, please visit my website at http://elizabethrosenovels.com. You can also follow me on amazon, facebook and other social media. Be sure to sign up for my newsletter so you won't miss sales, free books, and new releases. You can do so by going to https://bit.ly/3aK66i2.

Until next time,
   Elizabeth Rose

242

ALSO BY ELIZABETH ROSE

Medieval Series:

Legendary Bastards of the Crown Series

Seasons of Fortitude Series

Secrets of the Heart Series

Legacy of the Blade Series

Daughters of the Dagger Series

MadMan MacKeefe Series

Barons of the Cinque Ports Series

Holiday Knights Series

Highland Chronicles Series

Pirate Lords Series

Highland Outcasts

Medieval/Paranormal Series:

Elemental Magick Series

Greek Myth Fantasy Series

Tangled Tales Series

Portals of Destiny

Contemporary Series:

Tarnished Saints Series

Working Man Series

Western Series:

Cowboys of the Old West Series

And More!

Please visit http://elizabethrosenovels.com

About Elizabeth

Elizabeth Rose is an award-winning, bestselling author of over 100 books and counting. She writes medieval, historical, contemporary, paranormal, and western romance. Her books are available as EBooks, paperbacks, and some audiobooks as well.

Her favorite characters in her works include dark, dangerous and tortured heroes, and feisty, independent heroines who know how to wield a sword. She loves writing 14th century medieval novels, and is well-known for her many series.

Elizabeth loves the outdoors. In the summertime, you can find her in her secret garden with her laptop, swinging in her hammock working on her next book. Elizabeth is a born storyteller and passionate about sharing her works with her readers.

Please be sure to visit her website at **Elizabethrosenovels.com** to read excerpts from any of her novels and get sneak peeks at covers of upcoming books. You can follow her on **Twitter, Facebook**, **Goodreads** or **BookBub.** Join Elizabeth's **newsletter** so you don't miss out on new releases or upcoming events.